STONE OF COURAGE

Abe Jones, nicknamed 'Feather-Fist' for his reluctance to fight, hits the jackpot when panning for gold in a secluded creek. But he is immediately swooped upon by Lynch Corbett and Len Dyson, two of the toughest outlaws in the territory, who drive him off his patch at gunpoint. Sylvia Drew, witness to the event, urges Abe to reclaim what is rightfully his. She reveals to him an ancient Navajo relic known as the Courage Stone — one fragment of which will banish fear and protect the bearer from danger . . .

JOHN RUSSELL FEARN

◆

STONE OF COURAGE

Complete and Unabridged

LINFORD
Leicester

First published in Great Britain in 1956
as
Feather-fist Jones by Jed McCloud

First Linford Edition
published 2016

A catalogue record for this book is available
from the British Library.

ISBN 978–1–4448–2787–3

Published by
F. A. Thorpe (Publishing)
Anstey, Leicestershire

Set by Words & Graphics Ltd.
Anstey, Leicestershire
Printed and bound in Great Britain by
T. J. International Ltd., Padstow, Cornwall

1

The only sound was the faint gurgling of the creek. The brilliant Arizona sun glanced upon it, setting it into a tumbling stream of diamonds — only in this case the answer was not diamonds, but gold.

Young Abe Jones just could not believe it. For nearly five years he had been a 'dirt-washer' in this region, living in a small wooden hut near the stream. For five years he had prospected in the water, had followed the busy creek to its source and panned in its waters summer and winter. His father had told him it sprang originally from a gold-bearing seam and that, at intervals, gold ore and dust was washed down in the waters. For five years there had been nothing but mud and grit and silt — but now!

'I'll be doggoned,' Abe Jones whispered, the dancing reflections of the sun on the water patterning his astounded young face. 'I reckon there ain't no doubt of it, neither.'

He swirled the old sieve-dish in his hands and the light caught the genuine glint of gold deposit. Not much, true, but enough to show it was there. Then for Abe the first shock passed. He carefully separated the gold from the dirt and put it into the leather pouch beside him. Then he scooped his pan into the water again — and yet again, bewildered by the El Dorado which came up each time. His father had been right then. There were times when this stream gave up its wealth, and he was the only man in the region who knew about it.

Or so he believed. Having never been interfered with all the time he had prospected he was entitled to think that his activities were his own personal affair. But in this outlook Abe Jones revealed his youth, his lack of true knowledge concerning the region around him. This particular territory was by no means populated entirely by law-abiding home-steaders and townsfolk. There were others — outlaws, nomadic men of the plains, killers indeed if a human life stood between them and easy money.

No, Abe Jones was not working alone. More than one outlaw passing along the rimrock high above the stream had paused and watched him at work. More than one outlaw had returned at intervals to see if any progress had been made. Any man familiar with the region knew that the transference of something from the pan to the leather pouch meant gold — and so far this had never happened, until now.

And Len Dyson was watching. He had arrived just in time to see the transference. The moment he did so he slid from his horse and drew it behind the rocks out of sight. Then he himself squatted down and watched the scene below intently. After a moment he wriggled backwards carefully and signalled to a man lower down the opposite slope. Thus summoned, the second outlaw dropped from the saddle and came up to join his comrade.

'Looks like I ain't bin chasin' rainbows after all,' Len Dyson commented. 'That critter down there's found gold, else I'm crazy. Reckon we'll watch him for a bit an' see what happens. Keep low in case he looks up.'

The second man nodded and together they wriggled into a position where they could watch the unsuspecting Abe far below, busy at the side of the creek. Three more times he transferred something from pan to pouch and the eager speed of his movements was a complete give-away.

'Get what I mean?' Len Dyson asked, grinning crookedly. 'The kid's too young t'be allowed all that wealth.'

'Jus' wot I wus thinkin'.'

A marshal, had he passed just then, would have considered these two a prize catch. Both of them — Len Dyson and Lynch Corbett — had their unlovely faces plastered on barns, posts, and outhouses the length of Arizona.

Both of them were wanted for hold-ups, train robberies, and plain murder. Abe Jones could not have been watched by two more unscrupulous scoundrels in the whole region.

'Come to think on it,' Dyson resumed, his eyes narrowed, 'it's about time there wus a pay-off to the wait we've had. We've had a bead on this guy for over two years now an' he ain't shown any signs of shapin' 'til now. Lucky we happened by.'

'Sure was — an' it don't look as if we'll run into much opposition neither. Frum where I'm sittin' 'e don't look more than eighteen.'

Lynch was wrong in his estimate. Abe Jones was twenty-nine, but much of the callowness of youth had still not left him. Most of his life had been secluded — first with his parents on the ranch — then by himself in his hut after the death of his parents. He hardly knew any world existed outside the creek and the little valley.

'What do yuh figger on doin'?' Lynch

5

asked presently. 'I reckon I could finish him frum here. He'd never know what hit him.'

'An' leave his body for somebody to find? Riders do pass this way, remember.'

'So what? We're already wanted for other jobs, so one more can't make much difference.'

'Mebby not, but that ain't the way to do it. Proper thing to do is stake a claim on this creek, then nobody else can touch it without gettin' the law on 'em. What we do is just that, but to be sure our friend down there doesn't happen to outride us to the claim office we'll give him a work-over.'

Lynch was looking dubious. 'All sounds mighty pretty, but y'seem to have forgotten that if we show our faces anywhere near Tucson, much less the claim office, we'll be run in. We ain't considered respectable citizens.'

'Yeah — ' Dyson rubbed his sandpapery chin. 'Yeah, I'd forgotten that angle. Okay, then there's another

6

answer. We'll give this guy hell — clear him right out of the region, and take over instead. In a few days we oughta have washed up enough gold fur us to be comfortable for a long time to come. An' when yuh've got money yuh can buy liberty an' anythin' else yuh want.'

'No proof this feller's alone,' Lynch pointed out. 'Mebby others in the shack down there — '

'And mebby not. We'd have seen them by now if there wus — more especially with gold lyin' around. I'm goin' to take a risk, an' I'm doin' it right now. Come on.'

Dyson rose and began to move swiftly down the slope: not a yard behind him came Lynch, both of them with a gun at the ready. So absorbed was Abe Jones in his task, and so frolicsome was the noise of the creek, he had no warning of the men's approach until Dyson spoke.

'Hold it, feller, and git up!'

Abe turned his head sharply, startled, and then slowly got to his feet. The sieve-pan dropped as he raised his hands.

'Okay, okay, y'can keep your hands down,' Dyson added. 'But don't try an' reach fur your hardware. This is t'be a nice, friendly little chat. If yuh was seen with your hands raised by somebody passin' along the rimrock it might look bad. See?'

'I — I reckon so.' Abe looked from one to the other. He did not need imagination to judge from the men's faces that they were outlaws. They for their part were noticing the smooth youthfulness of Abe, the lack of hard-bitten lines usually chiselled into the visage of the men of the West.

'Looks like yuh found gold around here, huh?' Dyson asked casually, glancing about him.

'No business of yours, is it?'

'Might be: ain't easy to tell. An' don't come back so quick on the smart talk or I'll kick your teeth out! Fur your information we know exactly what yore doin' 'cos we've been watchin' yuh for a long time. Now, you've found gold it's time we took it over.'

'Time you what?' Abe repeated in amazement. 'By what right do you think you can do that? I live in this region and this creek is my property — '

'Legally?' Lynch interrupted, his eyes slitting.

'Not on paper, if that's what you mean. It's just mine by right of me bein' here — '

'Well, then, I reckon that makes it simple,' Dyson grinned. 'Just don't matter who's here since you've no legal claim. Might as well be us as you — '

'Now, look — ' Abe began angrily, but Lynch's harsh voice cut him short.

'We're lookin', kid, and there ain't anythin' interesting. Yore just plain finished around here — includin' your shack. Now grab yuhself a cayuse and git outa here.'

'I'll be darned if I will!' Abe clenched his fists. 'I've worked years for what I've got. I don't aim to be thrown out by a couple of no-account gun-hawks.'

9

Dyson tightened his lips. Deliberately he put his gun away — after making sure he was still covered by Lynch's six-shooter. Going forward he slammed out his right fist. The unexpected blow landed on Abe's jaw and knocked him backwards into the stream. The next thing he knew Dyson was dragging him up by his shirt collar.

'I don't play too rough with lily-whites,' Dyson explained contemptuously. 'That clip on the jaw was just to warn you to do as yore told or else get beaten up! Now git on yore way — an' don't ever come back.'

Abe hesitated, his fists still clenched. Dyson admitted to himself that he was vaguely surprised at the way Abe was taking it. He had expected a battle, even gunplay, but Abe did not attempt either. He seemed to be trying to make up his mind about something — then finally he relaxed and sloshed out of the stream. Without a word, his shoulders drooping, he made his way towards the shack.

'Better keep after him,' Lynch muttered, as Dyson came up. 'He may pull a fast one — '

'I reckon not. The critter's plain scared to Hades. Mebby he's lived too long by himself. We've had a few easy snatches, Lynch, but this is easier than any of 'em.'

They kept a few yards behind the dejected Abe, prepared for anything he might spring — but he did nothing more than release and saddle his mare in the nearby stable, a makeshift affair surrounded by a tumbledown fence.

'What about food?' he asked finally. 'No tellin' when I might need some. There's the water barrel wants filling too.'

'Go ahead,' Dyson ordered, jerking a thumb. 'Lynch 'll see you don't try anything.'

Methodically, Abe did that which was permitted him. Finally he was ready. He patted his single gun, then swung to the saddle.

'You don't reckon you can get away with this, do you?' he asked bitterly.

'We've got away with tougher things than this, lily-white. Only thing that can stop us is you shoutin' your face off when you arrive in the nearest town. Better not do that: We'll be out gunnin' for you if you do.'

'Granted you get the chance,' Abe retorted.

There was a momentary silence, then Lynch snapped: 'Git off that horse!'

'Huh?' Abe looked surprised; and so for that matter did Dyson. Lynch went on fiercely: 'Ain't no sense givin' this feller too much rope, Dyson. Yore gettin' kind-hearted in yuh old age an' that ain't goin' to do nobody any good. Let him walk to wherever he's goin' — without food or water. I'll gamble he'll never reach the next town in any condition to say anythin'. By that time, even if he can speak, we'll have raked off all we want. Go on, git off that horse!'

'You can't do this!' Abe shouted, dropping to the ground. 'You know as well as I do that it's plain murder to turn a man loose in the desert. It's nearly thirty miles to the next town!'

'All the better,' Dyson grinned. 'Thanks, Lynch, for remindin' me I wus gettin' soft — ' He strode forward, relieved Abe of his gun, then gave him a shove. 'Start walking — an' keep goin'. If you're not outa sight in twenty minutes we'll follow an' give yuh a start off yuh'll never forget.'

Abe hesitated. Again that queer look of fear and indecision came into his eyes; then he turned away and began walking. In silence the two gunhawks watched him go, and indeed they never took their eyes from him as he waded across the creek and then began to slowly climb the slope on the opposite side.

'Takes it meek, don't he?' Lynch grinned. 'Never seen a guy so easy to handle. I wus expecting plenty of hard work.'

'Yeah — ' Dyson took his eyes from Abe's departing figure at last and turned to the nearby pouch still lying beside the creek. When he poured the contents out into his palm he gave a whistle.

'Hell!' Lynch breathed, over his shoulder. 'This creek sure is a bonanza, and then some! Time we got busy seein' how much more there is, isn't it?'

They turned immediately to the task, quite unaware that up on the rimrock the one chance Dyson had forseen had come to pass. A passing rider had seen everything, from the moment they had held up Abe Jones beside the creek. The passer-by still watched — a young woman with the flowing chestnut hair and keen dark blue eyes of the true Westerner. A girl of outdoors, her skin tanned to deep gold. Not that she was a stranger in these parts. Her home was the Bar-19 ranch some five miles away and her father, the owner of the ranch, was one of the biggest cattle barons in the district.

One thing alone had attracted the girl to this point — the two lone horses of the gunhawks tied loosely to the rockspurs. From the lower trail, along which she had been passing on nothing more important than a morning canter, she had seen the horses, riderless and alone. What more natural than that she should investigate? — chiefly with the thought that somebody might be in trouble.

Somebody was — Abe Jones. Her eyes were hard with anger at what she had witnessed. Though she had not heard the words exchanged the movements she had witnessed had told her the whole story. Now she sat astride her horse and reflected, taking care to keep well back in the rocks to avoid detection.

She had a gun — a small serviceable automatic — but she knew better than try her prowess against such hardened characters as those below. On the other hand she could ride back home, tell her law-abiding father what she had seen and bring him and the boys back to investigate. But during that time the gunhawks could move on and vanish — so also could the young man, whose name she did not know. If he was heading for the desert, as he seemed to be, he could very soon be swallowed up.

Sylvia Drew did not hesitate any longer. She swung her horse's head and in a matter of moments was speeding along the lower trail, completely out of sight of the men in the valley. Before very long she reached the forbidding pass which gave direct entry to the expanse of the desert. Here she drew rein and looked around her, shading her eyes from the fierce glare of the sun.

At first she could not detect anything in the shimmering heat-waves, dancing away across the yellow sea to the horizon — then at length she caught sight of a slowly moving speck in the distance. Instantly she spurred her horse and five minutes later she had caught up with Abe Jones' slowly tramping figure. He stopped in surprise at beholding the girl. Staring at her he wiped the streaking perspiration from his face with his shirt sleeve.

'Howdy,' he said briefly. 'Quite a

vision in the frying pan!'

The girl dropped from her horse and came over to him. Like the outlaws, she had some difficulty in judging Abe's age.

'I'm Sylvia Drew,' she explained. 'Probably doesn't mean anything to you, but I saw what happened down at the creek.'

'Oh? You did?' Abe was still looking at her in wonder.

'Now you're probably wondering why I didn't interfere? Well, it didn't seem to me that one girl against two gunhawks like that would stand much chance. But if there was a plain steal of a man's property that was it! I assume you own that shack by the creek?'

'Sure I do, but I reckon a man don't own anythin' when two guns are pointing at him.' Abe tugged off his hat suddenly and gave a sheepish smile. 'Sorry, ma'am. Forgettin' my manners, I guess. My name's Abe Jones. Usta call me 'Feather-fist' when I was a kid. I reckon it'd still be appropriate.'

The girl looked puzzled. 'Why?'

'I'd rather not go into that: you might get the wrong idea an' think me yellow. I wouldn't want you to have that impression.'

Sylvia hesitated. 'Er — just as you wish. Anyway, I rode out here to give you a hand. It looks to me as though you're heading into the desert without water, food, horse, or ammunition. That's plain suicide — or don't you know?'

'Sure I know, but when you're told to get on your way and not come back unless you want shooting up, what else is there to do? I can only head for the nearest town. I don't know of any ranches close by — '

'Mine isn't so far — or rather my dad's. He's Tom Drew, the well known cattleman. Heard of him?'

Abe shook his head. 'I hardly would. I've lived so long by the creek, on my own, I just don't know what neighbours I've got — an' you don't learn much on an occasional ride into town for chow and necessities. And before I forget, I'd

18

like to say I appreciate your chasing after me like this. Nothing so nice has happened to me for years.'

'And it doesn't end right here,' the girl decided. 'I'm taking you back to my ranch. You can explain to dad how you were robbed of your property and he'll probably have a good answer ready. This is a job for a marshal, you know.'

'I s'pose so,' Abe admitted. 'I'd no ideas on that. I was just figgerin' to keep on walking and hope I'd reach town before I passed out.'

The girl jerked her head. 'Come on, my horse is tough enough to carry the pair of us.'

She swung easily into the saddle and Abe leapt up behind her. He said no more as she got the horse on its way. The whole thing had caught him so much by surprise he had not yet sorted himself out. The last thing he had expected was the arrival of a pretty and determined girl to help him.

'I'm a bit surprised,' she said, as they sped along, 'that you let those hombres get away with it so easily. You had your gun in the early stages: why didn't you take a chance and use it?'

''Cos I didn't have the nerve. I know that sounds bad in an open-air man, but it's true. It isn't that I'm a coward. It's just that I can't bring myself up to fighting point. That's why I got the name 'Feather-fist'. I can't even start to fight, never mind win a battle.'

Since Sylvia did not pass any comment Abe wasn't sure how she had taken it. Actually, she was trying to reason out why a young man of reasonably good physique should be so slow on the draw. It intrigued her feminine instincts: this was something she was determined to analyse.

In fifteen minutes they were speeding through the gates of the Bar-19 and into the big yard. Abe quickly slid from the horse and helped the girl down. He decided he liked the personal contact more than somewhat; then he followed her across to the big rambling ranch-house, beyond the screen door and into the big living room.

'Oh, there you are, dad! Glad you're about — '

A powerfully built, grey-headed man rose from the desk beside the sunny window. He was craggy, good natured, and obviously nobody's fool. Immediately his sharp grey eyes moved to Abe and summed him up.

'Meet Abe Jones,' the girl smiled. 'There's quite a story attached to him, dad, and I want your advice. In fact we both do.'

'Howdy,' the big fellow smiled, and Abe tried not to wince at the crushing handgrip. 'What's it all about? I can be pretty sure that it's genuine trouble otherwise my daughter wouldn't be mixed up in it. She's always trying to help somebody.'

'A mighty fine virtue,' Abe found himself saying; then he waited in somewhat self-conscious silence for the girl to carry on. She did so, without hesitation, giving every detail as she had seen it from her vantage point on the rimrock.

'And you don't know who they were, Mr Jones?' Drew asked tugging out his pipe.

'No; I'd never seen 'em before — but I do remember one of them was referred to as 'Lynch'. They looked like a couple of outlaws, but if there's a reward out for them I probably wouldn't see it. I don't get around much.'

'Lynch, huh?' Drew gave a grim smile. 'There sure is a reward out, boy. It'd probably be Lynch Corbett and his partner Len Dyson, two of the biggest hold-up men and murderers in the district.' Drew glanced at the girl. 'You were too far away to identify them, Sil?'

'Afraid I was, but even at that distance I could see they looked a couple of killers. Right now they'll still probably be panning at the creek, stealing gold that rightfully belongs to Abe Jones here. What do you think we should do?'

'That,' Drew said, lighting his pipe slowly, 'takes thinking about.'

Sylvia stared at him. 'What! Plain robbery doesn't need thinking about: it demands quick action. I'm all for getting the boys of the outfit to ride out there and beat the daylights out of those two killers — even to run 'em in to Tucson and collect the reward if need be.'

'That you're still young, my girl, is obvious by the way you talk,' Drew commented, looking at her solemnly through the tobacco smoke. 'If it comes to a legal showdown, those two men have as much right to get gold out of the creek as Abe Jones has. He has no legal claim on it; he just happened to be there and, by the unwritten law, entitled to lift all the gold he could as long as he was able. If bigger sharks came along and drove him off it's just too bad — but there's no legal restraint anyway.'

'Oh, legal restraint be darned!' Sylvia cried hotly, but her father shook his head.

'It's the mightiest weapon there is, my girl — stronger even than a gun. We can't bring a marshal into this because there's no real case. And we can't man-handle those men because we've no legal right to do so — '

'We've the legal right to nab them as wanted men!' Sylvia insisted. 'That's good enough excuse for getting our boys to deal with them.'

Drew considered this for a moment and then looked at Abe again.

'That shack beside the creek? I suppose it's your own?'

'The shack is, yes, but I've no claim on the land on which it stands. I just built there because it suited me. My father taught me all there is to know about building.'

'I see.' Drew gave a shrug. 'From the legal side we can only deal with these men if they enter that shack: then we can nail them for trespassing. On the illegal side we can adopt your idea, Sil, and have them run in as wanted men — and once you do that what happens?'

'Why, Abe Jones returns to his rightful possession of the creek,' the girl responded, spreading her hands.

'It isn't his rightful possession, Sil:

that's what we've been arguing about. And don't forget that he wouldn't be alone in trying to get gold once our boys had nailed those two outlaws.'

'How — how do you mean?' Sylvia was frowning.

'I mean that all the boys in our outfit would know there was gold in that creek, and they'd also know that it was there for the picking up, with no legal restraint. They'd be on to it like vultures on to a carcase.'

'I don't believe it!' Sylvia declared in scorn. 'They're all decent, law-abiding boys. They wouldn't dream of taking any gold.'

'No?' Drew gave a grin and shook his head. 'Men who ignore gold when it's there for the picking-up are few and far between, m' girl. Why do you think gold rushes started in the past? No man is truly honest in face of the yellow metal. The only deterrent would be a legal claim, and you'd have to file it in Tucson, Mr Jones. That would make your stake in the part of the creek — and the land over which it runs — entirely your property.'

Abe looked troubled. 'I guess I couldn't do that. The gold isn't always to be found in the same part of the stream. To do the thing properly my claim would have to cover the stream from its source, including the land over which it flows. I haven't the money for a payout as large as that. I've only just begun to find gold, remember — in anything like quantity, that is. And now even that's been stolen from me.'

Drew sighed. 'Which makes it mighty tough for you, Mr Jones. You mean that thanks to these gunhawks you haven't even got any gold at all?'

'Only a little, from odd spots in the last few days. Things had really started to happen this morning when the outlaws showed up. I don't really know whether it's worth making a fuss or not,' Abe finished moodily, and Sylvia stared at him.

'But you can't let them get away with it!'

'I don't see why not. They won't stay long for fear of being caught. The moment they've panned enough gold they'll be on their way. When that happens I'll go back. There'll be plenty more gold deposits washed down in that stream long after the gunhawks have gone.'

'Yes. I see what you mean.' There was a curiously contemptuous look on Tom Drew's face. 'Don't mind my saying this, Mr Jones, but it does look to me though this is all your own fault. Out here, as you ought to know, a man fights for his possessions — even to dying for them if need be. I gather you had a gun with you, until it was taken from you just before you left. Why didn't you try and use it? Shoot it out, if need be? If you'd killed either or both of those men the law would have been lenient. A man has a right to protect his valuables and himself.'

Abe fingered his hat brim and looked away. 'Well — I — somehow I didn't seem to get around to it. The dice were loaded pretty heavily on their side.'

'So you let them tell you what to do and then walked out into the desert? Where you'd certainly have died if my daughter had not chased after you. All things considered, Mr Jones, I think this is one problem you'll have to sort out for yourself.'

With that Drew turned back to his desk and resumed the correspondence upon which he had been engaged when the two had come in upon him. Sylvia hesitated, then, evidently thinking better of what she had intended saying, she motioned with her head to Abe and he followed her out on to the porch.

'Sorry we couldn't do better than that, Mr Jones,' she apologised. 'Dad's not seen it in quite the way I thought he would.'

'You can't blame him,' Abe smiled. 'He's got me down as yellow — as not being man enough to fight for myself, and on the face of it he's got every justification.' He sighed and looked moodily across the yard. 'Thanks for everything, anyway, Miss Drew. I've got just about enough money with me to buy a horse if you sell me one. Then I'll be on my way.'

'To where?'

'I dunno. Nearest town I can find, and where it's cheapest. In a week or two I'll ride back to the valley and see how things are. If the outlaws have gone I'll pick things up where I left off and call the interval a dead loss.'

There was a brief silence, then Abe became aware of the girl beside him, leaning as he was against the porch rail. Turning to look at her he realised for about the twentieth time what a pretty, honest-looking girl she was.

'Look, Abe — ' She laid a hand on his arm. 'Don't mind me cutting out the formality of 'Mr', will you? Look, if I got you a couple of forty-fives and rode back with you would you shoot it out with those boys? I'd help you. Between us we'd probably clean them up. I'd take the gamble.'

Abe shook his head. 'No. You might get yourself hurt and I wouldn't want that.'

'That sounds very nice, Abe, but is it the truth?'

Abe gave her a direct look. Her dark eyes were fixed on him.

'Well, let's say half of it,' he muttered. 'Like I told you before, I'd be too scared to tackle the situation.'

'Thanks for being so frank. I could pitch into you for being scared, but I'm not going to. What you need is help, otherwise everybody is going to take advantage of you throughout your life.'

'Could be — but I don't see there's much anybody can do about it. Matter of temperament.'

'Not entirely. Matter of outlook would be more like it. And I still think I can help you. For the moment forget about the outlaws and stay here, at least for a few days — '

'With your father in the mood he is? I'd feel pretty uncomfortable, believe me!'

'You don't have to. Dad will be quite nice, even if he can't alter his personal opinions. Besides, I think he'll have reason to change his mind in a while, and that's something I wouldn't miss.'

'About me?' Abe laughed dubiously. 'It just isn't possible.'

'We'll see. Now come with me and I'll show you where you can freshen up. You've lived by yourself so long, Mr Abe Jones, you need somebody to take you in hand — and I flatter myself that I'm the one to do it.'

2

In the main the girl's prediction concerning her father seemed to be correct. He apparently had no objection to an addition to the household, and throughout lunch he was as agreeable as anybody could be — unless it was that he did not dare to appear anything else now his wife — a huge, friendly, red-faced woman — had come into the picture. Whatever the answer, Abe did not feel nearly as uncomfortable as he had expected.

Once the lunch was over the girl came out with a surprising suggestion — made privately when she and Abe were on the porch to enjoy an after-lunch drink.

'Did you ever hear of the Courage Stone?' she asked slowly.

'The what?' Abe frowned at her from the basket-chair. 'Why, no. Can't say I ever did. What is it?'

'It's supposed to be a relic left behind by the Redskins — or at any rate the Navajos — when they were in this territory. Legend has it that all Redskins have touched the Courage Stone at some time in their lives, or else carried bits of it with them as jewels. It is supposed to make the person concerned devoid of fear and protects them from all dangers.'

Abe grinned. 'Sounds like typical Indian superstition to me.'

'I wouldn't be too sure of that, Abe.' The girl was looking thoughtful as she stared into the distance. 'I've seen many strange developments following a handling of the Courage Stone. I've even seen severe illness instantly cured. Whether it's a matter of faith, or something inherent in the stone itself, I wouldn't know but things have happened.'

'Which is building up to what?' Abe asked.

'I was merely wondering if it could

do for you what it has done for others — destroy that inferiority complex you seem to have. I believe it could. I've heard it said that Redskins are not so brave and stoic because it is their natural temperament, but because practically every one of them has had a dealing with a tribal Courage Stone at some time in his life.'

Abe reflected. 'Mmm, sounds interesting. I'll try anything once, even though I still believe it's a lot of superstitious nonsense. Where is there such a stone?'

'I can show you this very afternoon. About ten minutes' ride or a leisurely hour's walk.'

'All right. What are we waiting for?'

Abe got to his feet and the girl rose beside him. In a moment or two they were on their way, wandering across the rich pasture land in the burning heat of the afternoon sun. For himself, Abe did not particularly care whether they ever found a Courage Stone or not. His particular interest was in the girl beside him, in the easy way she talked, in the charm of her carefree personality. After having spent so many years fending for himself it seemed oddly like a very pleasant dream to have Sylvia beside him. Even more intriguing was the fact that she was obviously determined to help him in every way she could — and that, Abe hoped, could at root only mean one thing.

The afternoon was well advanced when, after several rests, they came to a stoney area far beyond the pasture region. Here there reared crumbled stone monoliths and obelisks, plainly the remains of some dead Navajo territory. In various places, defaced by climatic conditions, there still stood weird idols and half rotten boarding traced in queer inscriptions.

'I reckon I've never seen this spot before,' Abe said, gazing around him. 'Mighty interesting.'

'Must have been at one time,' Sylvia agreed. 'I've been here many a time. As a little girl I used to come with two girls from a neighbour ranch and we spent hours enjoying ourselves in these ruins and exploring the catacombs beneath. I know the place like the back of my hand. Follow me, and you can see a Courage Stone for yourself.'

She turned and Abe kept behind her as she picked her way amidst the ruins. It was plain from the way she detoured and gave warnings of danger areas that she knew every inch of the area. So eventually she paused at a flight of crumbled steps leading downwards.

'Hold on,' Abe said, as she began to descend. 'We'll need a light, won't we?'

'No. Most of the tunnel roof has crumbled away and light gets through quite brightly. You'll see.'

Abe did, in another minute or two. The short walk they took along a low tunnel revealed myriads of light-shafts stabbing through from holes above — a twilight radiance which also existed in the main underground room into which they presently came. From the look of the place, and judging from the still

36

untouched sarcophogi lying around, Abe assumed it was an old time burial vault.

'And here,' the girl said, halting, 'is a Courage Stone.'

Abe turned. He had been studying the sarcophogi. The girl was standing beside an eroded column, perhaps three feet high, on the flat top of which stood what appeared to be a chunk of rock. Abe crossed to it and then frowned.

'That's it?'

'Uh-huh.'

'But it looks the same as any rock anywhere. What's so unusual about it? I expected something like — like a gigantic ruby mebby. Anything but a piece of rock like that.'

'All I know is that that's it. Been here for ages.'

Still looking and feeling vaguely doubtful Abe fingered the stone experimentally. He failed to detect any change in his physical responses. No racing of the heart, no sudden upsurge of the emotions. The thing felt the way it looked — like a chunk of rock.

'Well, okay, if you say so,' he said finally, peering at the girl in the dim light. 'I still don't feel as David must have done when he went out to meet Goliath.'

'As far as I know,' the girl responded, 'the effect is not instantaneous. Takes time — and you'd do better if you had a piece of the stone always with you. Why not? Can't do any harm even if it doesn't do any good.'

'And suppose anybody finds the stone has been hacked about? I take it that Navajo descendants come here occasionally? I don't want a horde of Redskins after me for desecration!'

Sylvia laughed outright. 'My, you have lived in the backwoods a long time, Abe! Navajos haven't been here for centuries, and what survivors there are are practically civilised. All this goes back to a dead age. Here!'

Making the decision for him she lifted the rock from the pedestal and then deliberately let it drop from her grasp. It hit the stone floor and immediately splintered. Not entirely, but enough to scatter chunks in various directions.

'There you are,' she said. 'Grab a piece.'

Abe found a comfortable-sized fragment and put it in his pants' pocket, then he gave the girl a look.

'Why just me? Don't you feel like taking a piece yourself?'

'I did — long ago. I've a piece at home. I'm prepared to swear that it's been the main cause of my having had a happy, healthy life up to now. As for fear, I never experienced it in any great measure. As yet you don't know me very well, but you'll discover I haven't one tenth of the fears of a lot of women.'

'I hope fortune gives me the chance to discover that,' Abe grinned; then his expression changed and he looked vaguely surprised. 'Say, I just realised something. I'd never have had the nerve to say a thing like that to a girl, in the ordinary way. Mebby there's something in the stone at that!'

The girl only smiled and then led the way out of the burial chamber. Soon they were back in the bright sunlight, blinking after the darkness. Abe had to admit — to himself for the moment — that he felt a good deal better in spirit than for some time. He did not know whether to attribute it to the girl's delectable company or the rock splinter in his pocket. Either way, he had the feeling that he didn't give a darn even if the sky fell down.

'There's something I'd like to ask you,' the girl said, as they wandered casually on their way back to Bar-19. 'Are you a good shot with a gun?'

'Average. Why?'

'In a while, when you decide to stand up for your rights and reclaim your gold-bearing creek, you'll be up against at least two of the fastest and most deadly shots in the territory — '

'Meaning the two outlaws that kicked me out?'

'Meaning them, yes. You've got to learn how to shoot faster than they can, how to draw whilst they're still thinking about it.'

'Okay — and I notice you're assuming that I'm going to try and get the creek back.'

'Of course you are. In a day or two you'll feel you have enough courage to attempt it — but you also need practical aid as well as a fast-shooter. I don't want to sound as if I'm boasting, Abe, but I'm a crack shot. Dad taught me every trick, just as if I were a boy. He's a great believer in self-protection. I could pass on everything I know to you — the flick of the wrist, the trigger finger, the draw-and-fire technique.'

'I couldn't imagine a nicer teacher,' Abe smiled. 'How soon do we start?'

'Immediately after the evening meal: there'll still be plenty of daylight left. I'm quite, quite determined, Abe, to see that you put yourself where you belong around here. I don't intend to see you kicked around by a couple of hoodlums who are only one jump ahead of a necktie party.'

And Sylvia kept her word. Immediately after the evening meal was over — around seven o'clock — she led the way resolutely into the yard and thereafter Abe found himself being trained by a girl who obviously knew every trick. In silent amazement he watched her amazing speed and accuracy and thereafter did everything in his power to emulate her. At the end of a couple of hours, practice the light was fading, but the improvement in Abe's technique was more than obvious.

'A few more days of that, Abe, and you'll be better 'n most gunhawks around here,' old man Drew commented, who had been smoking his pipe and silently watching. 'I never knew Sil was quite so good as that. You've got a nice twist of the wrist, boy, and that's what counts.'

'A few more days?' Abe repeated. 'Am I to gather from that that you've no objection to my stickin' around for a while?'

'Objection? Why should we have?'

'Well I — I'd sort of gathered the idea that you think me something of a coward to let those two outlaws get away with it — an' there's no worse stigma in this part of the world than to be branded as yellow.'

Drew shrugged. 'I reckon that's true enough, boy, but in your case you might be just naturally nervous and not a real coward. Your sort needs bringing out, an' from what I've seen of Sil's activity the 'bringing out' is doing quite nicely. Don't worry about a thing: yore more than welcome to stop.'

'If I do I'd prefer to pay my way. Call it independence if you like, but — '

'Pay nothing!' Drew snorted. 'I can invite a guest to my own house, can't I?'

So Abe said no more. Apparently he had been enfolded into the bosom of the Drew family, and chiefly because of the attraction of Sylvia he was not going to make any bones about it. So he stayed on, day after day, learning marksmanship, enjoying Sylvia's company, gradually becoming aware that he was far much less reticent in his approach to life than he had been before, though how much of this was due to the friendly influence of the Drew family and how much to the chunk of Courage Stone he carried in his pocket he did not know. As for the two outlaws in the valley, he had almost forgotten all about them and the wealth they had literally swiped from him.

But they had not forgotten him. As day followed day after they had ordered Abe out into the desert they began to wonder. They had fully expected that he would return, probably with a marshal or else gun-toting friends far more tough than himself. Neither of these things had happened. They were left in peace and had three bags of gold deposit to show for their ceaseless work at the creek.

'I don't get it, Lynch,' Dyson commented, nearly a fortnight after Abe had gone, when he and his partner were panning beside the stream. 'An' it's that mug we kicked outa here that

I'm talking about. This sort of bonanza is too good to be true: I can't figger why we're left to work it.'

'Yeah.' Lynch narrowed his eyes at the sun-sparkled water. 'I've bin kinda wonderin' about that meself. I ain't a guy who likes peace — darned sight too dangerous. Gimme action every time an' you know what yore doin'.'

'Since both of us feel the same way there may be sump'n in it,' Dyson mused.

'Somethin' in what?'

'Instinct, if yuh like to call it that. The both of us is on edge, an' I've always figgered that's a kind of warnin' that there's trouble comin'.'

Lynch was silent for a long time. The intricate processes of instinct were entirely beyond his cloddish grasp, but he could dimly see that there might be something in what his brighter partner said.

'Could be,' he admitted. 'So what do we do about it?'

'Git outa here while the gittin's good.'

'You loco? An' leave all this golden

stream behind?'

'We c'n always come back when we're dead certain the way's clear. We've got enough right now in these pouches to put us on velvet fur a long time to come — one an' a half pouches of gold dust each. That'll amount to plenty of greenbacks when we get the stuff weighed at the assayer's.'

'Yeah, mebby — but I don't like the idea uv quittin'.'

'Better'n a bullet from somewheres when we ain't expectin' it.' Dyson got to his feet and looked around him on the peace of the valley. 'I'm tellin' yuh, Lynch, we're goin'. Ain't safe any more. Git the bedrolls from the shack an' we'll start packin'.'

'Okay — but first we'll separate these gold bags. Equal shares. I guess I don't trust you any more'n you trust me.'

Dyson scowled but made no comment. As carefully as possible, since they had no scales, they weighed out the gold deposit into equal quantities, which finally resulted in two well-filled pouches apiece.

'If there's more one way or the other when we git to the assayer we'll work it out,' Dyson said. 'Satisfied?'

'I reckon so — an' it ain't goin' to be easy to find an assayer. First town we show up in we'll be nailed. Don't forgit there's a price on us.'

'I know. I've thought that one out. Best we can do is head fur Mountain's End — 'bout twenty-five miles to the south.'

'Never knew there was such a place.'

'Well there is. In the shack there the kid must ha' made a lot of rough maps of the district. I've bin a-lookin' through some of 'em an' Mountain's End is clearly marked. Seems he usta git his chow from there — or mebby you didn't notice some of the hoss food bags had 'General Stores, Mountain's End' printed on 'em?'

'Nope.' Lynch looked vacant. 'I didn't.'

'Sounds to me like one of them backwaters where we'll be more or less safe — not a big place like Tucson that's crawling with law officers. We'll risk it anyways, and if we run inter trouble it won't be the fust time we've shot ourselves out of it. Okay, we start packin'.'

Lynch nodded and followed his partner across to the shack. Though in actuality there was no danger threatening them — apart from the workings of their own consciences and fear for their skins — Dyson was so convinced of approaching trouble he allowed no let-up in the preparations for departure. In a matter of fifteen minutes their few belongings had been gathered, the water barrels filled and the remainder of Abe's dwindling provisions appropriated, then the pair started out of the valley and headed for the desert, turning due south.

'Once we hit Mountain's End whadda we do?' Lynch asked, as they rode steadily in the torrid sunlight.

'Same as anybody else when there's money to work on. We start buyin' ourselves a little power. Purchase some property mebby, and gain a small hold. Then we build it up frum that. You'll see. Reckon you ain't got the brains to figger it out. Just leave that to me.'

Lynch shrugged. 'Okay. I'll tell yuh later whether I like yuhr notions or not — '

Which, to Dyson, made no odds. He was quite prepared, if it suited his purpose, to dry-gulch Lynch at any moment and use his share of the gold. The only reason he didn't was because Lynch was an expert with his gun, and always useful in a tight corner. Outside that he was just baggage. Not that Lynch himself had any illusions, either. He was always on the razor-edge of expectancy, ready for the moment when his treacherous partner would turn on him with the lightning speed of a rattler.

So these two unholy partners rode on their way, oblivious to the blaze of the sun, the cobalt sky, the hot wind blowing in their faces. Nor for the occasional beauty which even the arid desert revealed. They thought of nothing but their own gain and safety, or the prosperity they could build up from the gold they had stolen from an innocent.

★   ★   ★

It was in the late afternoon when they finally rode into Mountain's End, a ragged little township on the edge of the desert, dominated on three sides by looming mountain range. His elbows resting on the saddle-horn, Dyson surveyed the scene for a moment or two, and then spat leisurely into the dust.

'We'd ride a long way, Lynch, afore we'd find a better hide-out than this. Look at it! 'Bout dead on its feet, I reckon.'

Lynch grinned and nodded. What few men and women there were around were moving lazily up and down the boardwalk, most of them apparently going to or coming from the general stores — or else the druggist's shop further up the main street. Everywhere there was an air of somnolence. Even

50

the teams dragging an occasional buckboard through the main street seemed half asleep. Perhaps it was not to be wondered at. The afternoon sun was merciless and beating down with all its fury upon the little township.

'I don't see any reward-dodgers on them sidewalk posts,' Lynch commented presently, 'so mebby we're safe enough.'

'Sure we're safe — an' there wusn't ever an easier bunch to git eatin' outa our hands. Yeah, an' there's an assayer's at the end of the street, next to the Naughty Lady saloon. Let's go.'

They nudged their horses forward and the idlers of the town watched them in dour interest — but nothing more. There was no hint in any of the expressions that the two had been recognised as wanted men. There was rather a certain astonishment that two sweat-stained travellers should wish to even visit such a cock-eyed hole.

At the assayer's the two stopped and left their horses at the tie-rack. When they emerged again they were grinning all over their ugly faces and the better off to the tune of some ten thousand green-backs between them.

'I've some two thousand more 'n you,' Dyson commented, 'but I reckon I'm entitled to it since I did most uv the thinkin'. Any argument?'

'Nope,' Lynch shrugged. 'I ain't worryin' just as long as you don't try an' pull a big double-cross sometime. If ever you think of it remember I c'n draw faster 'n you — ' He looked about him. 'Well, we got this fur. What's next?'

'Make ourselves comfortable, of course, and then figger the best thing to do. There's a real estate chiseller across the street there: mebby he can put us in the way of buyin' some property. Fur the moment Ma Wentworth's roomin' house down the street looks promisin'.'

Quite promising, as events turned out. Even though the ample Ma Wentworth didn't particularly like the look of her new potential lodgers the money they carried held plenty of conviction. Before long their horses were in the private stable and they themselves had a double bedroom to themselves.

'An' no shavin',' Dyson said, as Lynch poured out a jugful of warmed water into the basin. 'We've grown plenty uv fungus down at the creek and we might do worse 'n keep it. Make it all the harder to identify us.'

'Sure thing,' Lynch assented. 'And that reminds me: if the folk get curious an' want to know what we are what's the answer?'

'We're cattlemen from up north. An' don't say anythin' about prospectin' otherwise we might start a stampede for the creek. I wouldn't put it past a dope like you to tell everything, specially when you've had a drink.'

Dyson said no more and in some disgust Lynch turned to the task of freshening up. So began their stay in Mountain's End. By evening time they were feeling at peace with the world. New clothes and hats, well supplied

53

with money and looking exactly what they pretended to be — fairly well-to-do cattlemen from up north. By this time they had also seen the real estate pedlar and emerged from his office with a list of properties. Some were small businesses in the 'town' itself and others were homesteads and ranches in the surrounding countryside. The prices of each were surprisingly low.

'Which means only one thing,' Dyson said, as he and Lynch sat in the Naughty Lady saloon that night over their drinks. 'This district must be as dry as a furnace. Probably no good watercourses and pasture mostly withered. Nope — we don't go for any of these spreads. 'Sides, there ain't much y'can make on an honest, legitimate ranch. Gotta be done in a big way to produce big profits. Plenty of graft on the side. Nope, what we want is somewhere where we can make the public pay for the privilege of buyin' frum us. Take a place like this, fur instance.'

Lynch looked around him on the

faded, heat-warped walls, the rusty, swinging lamps, and finally the back-bar mirrors which were badly in need of resilvering. In spite of the fact that the place was generally decrepit the custom was good. Men and women were crowding the tables and around the bar, whilst in the smaller adjoining room the clicking of the faro and roulette tables bespoke a good trade.

'I got it!' Dyson declared abruptly. 'Right here, Lynch, there's the heart uv Mountain's End, as yuh might say.'

'The heart?' Lynch had his vacant look back again.

'That's what I sed. Run a joint like this an' yuh've got the people right where you want 'em. They've got t'have a saloon: it's the one thing that can't be done without in this part of the world. Once yuh've got 'em here you can make money fast. Fixed gaming tables, special mixed drinks that don't cost a cent to make but which we can charge anythin' fur — an' what's more y'can be in the centre of everythin', making all the useful contacts y'want.'

'Contacts?'

'Yeah, sure. Yore more'n a mite dumb tonight, ain't you? Money's made by havin' the right contacts to fix whatever deals you want, an' the place where all contacts come together is usually the gin palace, like this. Time we went into this. Given a few months runnin' a place like this an' bringin' it up to date, we could have the whole control of Mountain's End in no time — an' would that be sump'n!'

Lynch was not sure whether it would or not. He hadn't the imagination or the drive of Dyson — so he swallowed the rest of his drink and sat morosely thinking. The next thing he knew a big fellow in a black suit and displaying a white shirt-front and shoe-string tie was standing beside the table.

'Howdy, gents,' he greeted affably. 'Was I right in thinking you are trying to catch my eye?' He looked at Dyson.

'You were,' Dyson acknowledged, struggling to get a little more polish in his thick voice. 'Yore the owner of this place, I s'pose?'

'I sure am — Grant Munroe's the name.' An enormous hand reached out and Dyson and Lynch shook it each in turn. Then Munroe sat down, his huge frame overspreading the narrow hard-back chair. He was darkly handsome in a clumsy kind of way. Black haired, big mouthed, with strong yellow teeth.

'Yore strangers around here?' he announced. 'What'll be your pleasure, gents?'

'Rye,' Dyson said, and Lynch mumbled 'Scotch'. Then when it had been brought Munroe fingered his own glass of gin and raised a verandah of an eyebrow.

'I s'pose you wanted me for somethin' important?'

'Yeah — very important,' Dyson acknowledged coolly. 'Nothing less than to ask if you ever thought uv sellin' this place? An' my name's Edgar Salter. I should ha' mentioned that. This is Cliff Gregson, my partner. We're both cattle men from up north — and in a big way too.'

'Glad to know you, gents. Sell this place, did you say?' Munroe grinned widely with all his teeth. 'Why should I when I'm sittin' pretty?'

'I thought mebby you could be prettier some place else if it was made worth your while.' Dyson shrugged. 'My partner an' I'd be prepared to buy. Wouldn't we, Cliff?'

'Well — er — ' Lynch hesitated before a mental vision of a disappearing five thousand dollars.

'Sure he would,' Dyson hurried on. 'He's always a bit slow in catching on, so I take the lead. Sure you ain't thinkin' again, Mr Munroe?'

Munroe was silent, staring into his glass and rubbing his huge chin. Finally he raised his big eyebrows again.

'Well, mebby I am due for a change at that. I've bin here a good few years now an' the wife's always askin' me to move on. That's one good reason why I haven't tidied this place up a bit. I guess you don't when yore thinkin' of being on your way at any moment.'

'Right here you've got a customer,' Dyson said calmly. 'What's your price?'

Long silence. Finally Munroe finished his drink and said, 'Sixty thousand dollars.'

'I'll give you fifty thousand, and no more.' Dyson looked quite calm about it. 'It'll cost the remaining ten thousand to bring the place up to scratch.'

Munroe hesitated. 'Yore on the level about this? Not just bargaining for the sake of it?'

'Dead square. I'll have the money within a week. It'll mean my partner and I ridin' back north first of all to make a few arrangements. In the meantime you get your lawyer to draw up the deed of transfer. That fair enough?'

On the face of it, it apparently was. Presently Munroe grinned.

'You're the type I like doin' business with, Mr — er — '

'Salter.'

'Yeah — Mr Salter. No frills, no nothin'. Okay, it's a deal. We'll drink on it.'

They did — not once but several times. At the end of an hour Munroe was pleasantly mellow and took his leave in the best of tempers. Within a week the deal was to be concluded.

'You plain loco?' Lynch asked moodily, rolling a cigarette. 'Where the hell do we get fifty thousand from? We've only got ten between us, an' I'm not partin' with my share fur nobody.'

'Yuh don't have to. What d'yuh suppose a bonanza creek's fur? We're going right back at sun-up and pan enough gold to pay fur this lot.'

'But I thought yuh sed we should get out 'cos you figgered there was danger or sump'n.'

'Sure I did, an' I still think that way — but with a chance like this we've got to risk whatever danger there is. We didn't know such an opportunity would drop into our lap. Once get our hands on this, Lynch, and the whole town 'll be ours afore you know it.'

3

According to plan, Dyson and Lynch left Mountain's End the following morning for the hard ride back to the creek, and it was while they were pursuing the desert trail that Abe Jones was also making up his mind to make a move. It was not that he felt he would outstay his welcome, but he knew quite well that the secure paradise in which he was dwelling was not of his own making and, in as pleasant a way as possible, old Tom Drew had already made this fact clear.

'Think I'll start headin' back for the creek, Sil — ' Abe came out with the decision when they were enjoying their usual rest on the porch after lunch. 'You an' your folks have bin more 'n kind to me but it can't go on for ever. Not as though I'm convalescent, or anythin', an' a man strong in wind and limb oughta be on the move.'

'As you wish,' Sylvia answered quietly. 'All I wanted was for you to feel more confident before launching off again. From the way you talk maybe you're feeling that way?'

'Yeah. I wouldn't know whether it's this chunk of Courage Stone I'm carrying around or whether it's your own personal influence but I sure don't feel half as leary as I used to.'

Sylvia smiled slightly. 'It's the Stone, Abe. No matter how much I may influence you personally I couldn't possibly change your nervous complex. Only the Stone could do that. Well, what do you propose doing? Have you thought it out?'

'You bet I have. I'm going back to that bonanza creek of mine and get as much gold out of it as I can — enough anyway to stake a full claim on it for future use. When I've got that far I won't be lackin' for money. That'll be the time to start planning what I do next.'

'Yes, but — ' Sylvia looked troubled. 'Look, Abe, you're not intending to bury yourself again in that lonely spot, surely? I'll never have an easy moment wondering how you're going on. You need company of some kind.'

Abe grinned. 'Only one kind of company I'd like, I reckon, and at this stage I can't afford it.'

'Afford what? It hardly takes a fortune to live in a shack and get a few provisions now and again, does it?' Sylvia checked herself and blushed slightly. 'Or perhaps I'm getting ways ahead of myself? Maybe you're not thinking what I'm thinking.'

'I'm thinking I'd love nothing better than to have you as my wife,' Abe said seriously, astonished at his own free tongue. 'But I'm not havin' any wife of mine living with a no-account prospector in one of the loneliest spots in the territory. I'm used to roughin' it but yore not. You've got everything you need here and every comfort. I wouldn't ask you to exchange that for my way of life. No, let me get some money together first then, if you're still willing, I can put you somewhere decent.'

Sylvia put a hand on his arm and looked at him intently. 'I suppose it didn't occur to you that it's only you I want? The money doesn't matter, and I can rough it as good as anybody if I have to. Even though dad isn't without money now there have been times when we've struggled hard. I can take it, Abe.'

Abe got slowly to his feet, his face clearly expressing that he couldn't take in the situation — until Sylvia had her arms about his neck and was kissing him earnestly.

'I'll be doggoned!' he exclaimed finally, holding her and staring into her face. 'That a gal as pretty an' sweet as you could fall for a no-account rabbit like me! It ain't possible!'

'Of course it's possible! It's happened! And don't pretend it's a surprise, either. You don't think I'd have helped you so much if I hadn't cared for you, do you?'

'I — I reckon I don't quite know what to say, Sil.'

'Then I'll say it for you. We're going to get married — this very week if possible. After that we go together to the shack and start on the job of building up the financial side. I can look after you properly — '

'Sure, sure — but if the outlaws are still there?'

Sylvia raised an eyebrow. 'Well? If they are?'

Abe looked at the .45 hanging in his gunbelt and then grinned.

'If they are they won't be for long! With you and a Courage Stone to back me up I could conquer the earth. Mebby I can even start livin' down that 'Feather-Fist Jones' monicker that's stuck to me so long — '

He broke off, uncertain of himself as old man Drew came strolling on to the porch, puffing contentedly at his pipe. Instantly he could sense the unusual in the atmosphere.

'Didn't interrupt anything, did I?' he asked dryly. 'I sort of had the impression the porch isn't private.'

'During this week, dad,' Sylvia said deliberately, 'Abe and I are going to be married. Then I'm going with him to the creek to pan for gold.'

Abe waited for it. He was prepared for a storm, a deluge of questions — almost anything. His eyes fixed on Sylvia's slim, determined young figure and he noticed the resolution in the set of her jaw — but her father did not take up the challenge. He merely grinned and settled in the wicker chair.

'Mebby it's about time,' he commented.

Sylvia stared at him for a moment, then hurried forward. Her arm went round his neck as she dropped to her knees.

'Then you're giving it your blessing, dad? That it?'

He looked into her excited face, unmoved. 'That's it, Sil. Matter of fact your mother an' I have bin wonderin' for quite a time how your life would work out. Not much fun for you here with us old folks, and you'd not much chance of making contact. Then out of a clear sky dropped Abe Jones here. With your help I reckon Abe might become a hundred per cent man one day. Don't get me wrong, boy,' Drew added. 'I know you've got a nervous complex — or did have. That ain't your fault. Sil's probably the one to help you get rid of it.'

'Mebby she's done it already,' Abe answered. 'I'm good an' ready anyhow to tackle those two down at my creek — an' I'm going this afternoon to see if they're still there.'

'And I'm coming with you,' Sylvia decided, getting to her feet. 'Just wait a moment while I tell mum the glad news — '

She vanished behind the screen doors. Abe gave old man Drew a serious look.

'I want you to know I'm mighty glad, boy, mighty glad,' Drew said. 'That's one fine girl yore getting.'

'You don't have to tell me, Mr Drew: I know it. An' I'll take darned good care I prove worthy of her. Right now I'm worryin' about her coming to the creek with me. If there should be some trouble an' shootin' I don't want her mixed up in it.'

Drew grinned. 'Before yore much older you'll learn that whenever Sil makes up her mind about a thing she does it, and there's nothin' nobody can do to alter it. Better let her have her head, boy, and go saddle the horses.'

Abe shrugged and went off down the porch steps. By the time he had got two horses saddled and ready from the stable the girl had rejoined him, her dark blue eyes still dancing brightly.

'I told mum, Abe, and she's every bit as pleased about it as dad! Oh, isn't it a wonderful day!' She hugged herself in delight.

'Sure is,' Abe admitted. 'Darned sight more wonderful than I ever figgered could be possible. Okay, up you get.'

He lifted her to the saddle of her mare and then swung up into his own saddle. In another moment they were on their way and Sylvia never stopped talking. Everything she saw was delightful. The whole world was nothing but beauty and sunbeams. Abe, deciding this was purely the natural reaction of a woman in love, only made a comment here and there — and finally neither of them said anything at all as they came over the rimrock crest of the valley and beheld two lone figures at work far below.

Abruptly the world had become a place of foreboding and grim reality once more.

'So they're still there,' Abe muttered, narrowing his eyes. 'From the look of 'em you'd say they'd never moved since the day I was slung out of here. Okay, if that's the way they want it.'

He dropped from the saddle, felt in his shirt pocket, then dragged his splinter of Courage Stone to light. He tossed it lightly up and down in his palm and grinned up at the girl.

'I reckon this is where we can put redskin superstition to the test,' he commented. 'You stay here, Sil: it might be dangerous. I'll handle this myself — '

'But I want to come!'

'Definitely not. I don't intend you to get in danger for a single instant.'

Drawing his solitary .45 he held it in readiness as he went cautiously down the slope — and down at the noisy creek Dyson and Lynch Corbett never heard his approach. They had in fact only been here half an hour themselves after the gruelling desert ride, and since every moment counted to get enough gold deposit together they had immediately set to work, so far without any spectacular results. The stream was apparently not so beneficent as it had been.

'Enjoyin' yourselves, boys?' Abe asked.

Instantly both men twirled. Dyson dropped the sieve-pan with a noisy clatter and his hand flew to his gun.

'Hold it,' Abe warned. 'The both of you.'

Lynch gave a crooked grin. 'See who it is?' he asked dryly. 'The mug we thought the desert had swallowed up. Mebby there was something in your instinct about danger at that.'

'Danger? From this lily-white?' Dyson laughed in scorn. 'All he needs is t'be shown he can't be playful with us.'

He strode forward arrogantly, regardless of the gun — but he checked himself and an ugly look spread over his face as he suddenly found his hat blown from his head.

'I'm not just talkin' for the sake of it,' Abe explained, moving leisurely forward. 'Draw on me or even step forward and I'll blast you — but good. Right now I'm back to claim what you took from me and y'can try the desert yourselves for a change.'

Neither man spoke. There could be no doubt in either of their minds that there was something very different about the young man from the previous occasion — unless he was trying to pull a bluff. And with only one gun.

Dyson grinned suddenly. 'Better put your peashooter away, Lily, before you get hurt. Yore not dealing with kids, remember — '

'I sed get on your way,' Abe repeated coldly. 'Hurry it up before I make the pair of you start dancing!'

That was enough for Dyson. He lunged forward suddenly, his right fist bunched. But before he had completed his strides foward a tearing pain went through that fist and he screamed with the unexpected anguish. Stupidly he looked at his hand, brimming with blood, then at the wisp of smoke curling from Abe's gun.

'You could have saved yourself that,' Abe said. 'Wash your hand in the stream and you' — he looked at Lynch — 'tie it up for him. Then fill your water barrels and get going. You can take your horses, which is more than you let me do. What gold you've collected you can leave.'

'We ain't collected any yet!' Dyson snarled, nearly dancing with the pain of his smashed hand.

'Don't hand me that! You've been stuck here nearly three weeks. In that time you must have found plenty of deposits. Where are they?'

'Changed into greenbacks,' Lynch answered quickly, as he saw the gun point in his direction. 'We've cashed in on what we got only it wasn't enough so we came back fur more —'

'Shut up, you hyena!' Dyson blazed at him. 'Do yuh have to tell him everythin'?'

'I reckon I do when he's on that end uv the gun!'

Abe grinned. 'You've a darned sight more sense than your partner, evidently. Hurry up and get that hand fixed.'

Muttering to himself Dyson turned to the stream and spent a few moments washing his wounded hand. It looked a good deal worse than it was. The bullet had gouged a trough across the upper part of his hand and produced plenty of torn flesh but no broken bone.

'I don't get this,' Lynch murmured, as he tied Dyson's neck scarf round the damaged hand. 'Do you reckon he was foolin' last time?'

'Nope. He wouldn't have gone so meekly into the desert if he wus. He's pullin' a bluff because he happened to draw fust — but he ain't going to get away with it. Look, I'm going to aim this pan-sieve at him. When I do, you draw and fire. Don't matter if you kill him: we'll git rid of him somehow,. We've got to get this gold. Right?'

'Okay.'

Abe did not hear what was being said but he watched intently. With all his alertness, however, he was not quick enough to grasp the trick with the sieve. He assumed Dyson was going to wash his hand at the stream again before the final tie-on of the scarf — and the next thing he knew the sieve-pan was flying straight at him. He dodged, but the pan struck him a glancing blow on the eyebrow and drew blood. Simultaneously Lynch's gun exploded and a tearing pain ripped through Abe's right arm.

'On him!' Dyson snapped, and with Lynch he charged forward.

Abe went down before the pair of them but to his satisfaction his right arm was still usable so evidently the bone was not broken. He lashed out with it, his fist smashing straight into Dyson's face and sending him sprawling. Up came his left boot and drove into Lynch's stomach, doubling him up.

The respite was brief but it was sufficient for Abe to get on his feet. He transferred his gun to his left hand and fired savagely. Lynch stared in amazement as the bullet whanged his own gun clean out of his hand. Though it was more accident than marksmanship it looked amazingly effective — enough for Lynch to turn and start stumbling away across the stream.

'Yeah, keep going!' Abe yelled after him. 'An' you too!'

He fired twice at Dyson, over him and around him, setting him dodging wildly — but Dyson was far more wily and tough than Lynch. He went to midstream, then wheeled and fired. It was so swift Abe had no chance to foresee it. He went down with a smashing pain in his shoulder. Dyson grinned widely and, encouraged, came swiftly forward, his gun ready. He levelled it, but before he could fire for the second time there was a gun report from higher up the slope and a bullet scorched his right knee. He gasped, staggered, and then stared at the figure of Sylvia racing down to where Abe had fallen. The sun glinted on the automatic in her hand but just at this moment her whole attention was concentrated on Abe.

And Dyson knew it. Gritting his teeth against the pain in his leg he took aim. The gun exploded and to Abe's horror he saw Sylvia — only a few yards from him — abruptly throw both her hands to her breast and then pitch forward into the dust and rockery. She rolled a few feet and became still.

Abe half struggled up and reached for his gun. Savagely he blazed away with it at Dyson's now limping, retreating figure across the stream — but the shots missed.

The cylinders empty, Abe took no trouble to renew them. He moved instead to where Sylvia lay and raised her head and shoulders in his arms. There was an ivory pallor about her face which he did not like, a tremendous heaviness in the weight of her body. It took him about ten seconds to absorb the awful shock. The girl was dead, the small bloodstain on her blouse the one clue where the bullet had driven straight to her heart.

For a moment or two the world stopped for Abe. He forgot the still retreating gunhawks; he forgot his own gun and cartridges. His whole mind was in a blur of grief, fury, and turmoil. In the brief time he had come to know Sylvia, she had come to mean everything in the world to him, and now it was over, finished. It was quite impossible for him to take it in. Then, very slowly, he became aware of blood soaking his sleeve from his own shoulder wound, of a small trickling from his cheek where the sieve-pan had hit it. These things were nothing as compared to the numbness of mind produced by the killing of Sylvia.

With a tremendous effort he forced himself to move. Awkwardly, because of his damaged shoulder, he drew the girl's dead weight into his arms and stumbled up the long slope back to the horses. Here he tied the reins of the girl's horse to his own mount and then clambered into the saddle, cradling Sylvia's body in his arms.

How he made the journey back to the Bar-19 he did not quite know. It had a nightmare quality, as though he were actually no part of it. His senses only began to vaguely register again when he rode into the ranch yard. Old man Drew was on the porch, dealing with correspondence at the small table, and enjoying the fresh air at the same time.

The moment he glanced up he realised something was wrong and came hurrying down the porch steps.

'She should never have come with me,' Abe kept whispering, in between incoherent explanation. 'I didn't want her to! I didn't want her to!'

'Take it easy,' Drew muttered. 'Give me a hand to carry the body inside. It's a weight.'

And in half an hour the body had been laid in Sylvia's room and Abe was seated in morose silence in the living room, staring straight before him. Equally silent were old man Drew and his wife. Mrs Drew was openly weeping but somehow Tom Drew kept a rein on himself.

'I'm riding over to Tucson to report this,' he said presently. 'Murder! We'll have the authorities pick up Dyson and Lynch and they'll get what's coming to 'em. They've already got half a dozen killings to answer for as it is.'

'If they've dodged the authorities so far they'll go on doing it,' Abe muttered, holding his roughly bandaged shoulder through his shirt. 'There's a personal grudge in this, Mr Drew! Those dirty hyenas killed your daughter and the girl who would have become my wife — leastways Dyson did. I regard him as my own especial prize. I'm going to follow him to the ends of the earth for this and rub him out.'

Drew shrugged. 'That's up to you, but I'm also going to advise Tucson. You'd better rest up a bit until you're better. You've taken a good beating on that shoulder, and then there's the shock of Sil too — '

'I'm all right,' Abe snapped, getting to his feet. 'I'm getting on the move right away before those skunks cover up their tracks too well. Last time I saw 'em they were heading into the desert without horses, and one of 'em — Dyson — with a damaged leg. They won't get far. Far or near I'm hanging on to them. I don't care if it means a necktie for me at the end of it for killing Dyson, but I'm going to risk it.'

'But, Abe — ' Drew began, then he gave it up as he realised Abe was not listening. He strode to the doorway purposefully and in another moment the screen door slammed behind him —

★   ★   ★

Two such men as Dyson and Lynch, ever mindful of their own comfort, were not the type to head into the hazards of the desert if there were any way of saving themselves. Neither of them had even left the valley but had stopped in the higher extremity of the slope and concealed themselves behind the rocks. It was from here that they had seen Abe's slow toil up the slope with Sylvia in his arms, and had witnessed his ultimate departure.

'I didn't even know there was a gal mixed up in it,' Lynch commented, puzzled. 'Where she come frum?'

'How the hell should I know?' Dyson snarled. 'All I know is she splintered my damned knee so I let her have it back. Frum the look of things I put her out of action.'

'Yeah — mebby killed her,' Lynch muttered.

'I ain't that good with a gun,' Dyson growled, gripping the bloodstained patch over his knee. 'Just creased her, I reckon.'

'To be hoped that's all it wus, otherwise that lily-white may be out gunnin' fur us — an' the way he's shapin' he could be more 'n a nuisance. Can't think what's happened t'him since we last had a brush with him.'

'You can't think at all,' Dyson observed sourly. 'Just the same he may make trouble, so we'd better get out while we can. He's out of the way at the moment so go and fetch our cayuses.'

'An' if he's simply waitin' to take a pot shot at me, what then?' Lynch's eyes were on the rise from which Abe had departed.

'We see'd him go, didn't we? I reckon there weren't no trick about that — but he could come back mighty fast so get the horses. I can't even hobble with this blasted leg. Let Lily-white's horse free.'

Lynch shrugged and did as he was told. When eventually he came back with the horses he asked a question.

'What about the gold we wus goin' to get? Don't we do it whilst we're right on the spot?'

'No.' Dyson was taut with pain. 'We might be on a spot uv another colour if we did. We're headin' straight back fur Mountain's End. Fur one thing I need a sawbones to fix this leg: for another I'm in no condition to tackle Lily-white if he decides to come back. That guy's become dynamite, even though I can't think why.'

'Then yore throwin' up the idea of that deal with Munroe?'

'I'm not throwin' up anythin' but I gotta get myself right first, ain't I? Gimme a hand.'

With difficulty Dyson managed to get into the saddle and he knew he would not be able to get off it until he fell off on return to Mountain's End. Lynch, not at all sure what the programme was henceforth, swung to his own horse and the pair of them made for the desert trail. Which was one reason why Abe, arriving back at the valley some half an hour after the gunhawks had left, failed to see them anywhere when he galloped his horse round the topmost of the valley and so came to the desert.

'Now just where did those critters get to?' he muttered, his eyes narrowed in the sun glare as he gazed around him. 'Oughta still be in sight if they're walkin', and one of 'em injured at that.'

Strangely, the possibility of them having returned for their horses never occurred to him right then, so he did not check up. Instead he continued riding swiftly into the desert until it began to dawn on him that they could be almost anywhere in this sun blistered immensity, especially on foot. He drew his horse to a halt and considered. To trail the two by footprints in the sand was impossible. It was too loose to retain footprints. Of course there might be blood spots here and there and from Dyson's wounded leg.

Abe hesitated no longer. He rode back quickly to the valley, and then into it, finally pausing at the spot where he had last seen the two men departing up the slope. The first thing he beheld was not blood-stains but the imprints of horses' hooves. Two sets of them travelling up the slope and then vanishing in the harder, rocky earth.

Abe tightened his lips. So the two had returned for their horses and ridden away on them, which meant they could be far away by now, and in any possible direction. To follow any trail through the desert was impossible, and in any case he himself had no provisions and water to make a protracted journey. The only thing he could do was return to the ranch and weigh up the possibilities as to which direction the two might have taken. Since they were both wanted men they would not be very likely to reveal themselves too much.

The only possibility Abe could think of was Mountain's End, the dozy little township which he himself so often visited. It might be worth a visit. If he guessed wrong he would have to wander far and wide until he located them — even if it took the rest of his life. Vengeance was the one thing upon which he was determined.

These were the various aspects he thought over as he rode slowly back across the base of the valley. With every moment now he was commencing to think more coolly. To achieve his purpose it would not be good sense to suddenly present himself. It would probably give the gunhawks time to go away. He had to plan something subtle, contrive a scheme whereby they would walk into a trap and be quite unable to escape. And that would take thinking about. The more he considered, the more it seemed to Abe that his best plan right now was to return to the Bar-19, attend Sylvia's funeral, and then talk things over with old man Drew. His mature commonsense might afford plenty of good suggestions. There might be some way, Abe decided, in which he could perhaps work hand-in-glove with the law officers of Tucson to bring in these two much-wanted men —

★　★　★

And in the meantime Dyson and Lynch continued their journey across the desert. Both of them fully expected evidences of pursuit and were prepared to shoot it out if it came to it — but the miles went by under the blazing sun and nothing happened. Until finally they had settled into a more comfortable frame of mind.

They did not delay at the water holes en route. The state of Dyson's leg made it necessary they keep on going, and a pretty weary, travel-stained pair they looked when finally they reached Mountain's End. With the help of Ma Wentworth's two hefty sons Dyson was lifted from the saddle of his horse and carried to the bed in his room whilst Lynch went for the local doctor. By mid-evening the cursing and bad-tempered Dyson had had the bullet removed from his leg and was more-or-less comfortable as he lay on the bed.

'I'll be darned if I c'n see what good it'll do us to stay on in this dump,' Lynch commented, turning from surveying the main street through the window. 'We certainly can't carry on with the Munroe sell-out.'

'It ain't necessary to pay fur everythin' in this world,' Dyson growled, dragging at his cigarette. 'I was prepared to do a straight deal with Munroe but since things haven't worked out that way mebby we want a change of plan.'

'No doubt uv it — but what?' Lynch sat on the solitary chair and gave a dubious glance.

'I've bin weighin' things up, and I surely don't have to tell yuh that this town is the sleepiest we ever gotten into. One strong man with a couple of six-shooters could hold the whole place t' ransom. Two strong men would make it a certainty.'

'Could be,' Lynch admitted. 'What are yuh driving at?'

'That we take over Munroe's joint by force. More 'n one small township in this territory has been taken that way, an' I'm willin' to try it. Since we're wanted by the law anyways it doesn't make much odds what more we do. We've only got one life each to give up if we fail. But we won't fail. Once git Munroe out of the way — since he's more or less the boss of the town at present — and the rest of the folks 'll just fall in line. They'll be too plumb scared t'do anythin' else.'

Lynch pondered. 'It's one hell of a risk. There might be a lot of good gunmen amongst these cowpokes and homesteaders. We might take on more 'n we could manage.'

Dyson propped himself on his elbow. 'Look, Lynch, we've gotta settle somewhere, and we've got to be in a position of power so nobody c'n question us.

89

This town is ways off the beaten track and once well dug in we could probably have many years of peace. We're near enough to that gold creek too to risk goin' back at a later date. I'm for a take-over at the point of the gun the moment this blasted leg of mine eases up.'

'And that'll be a week, according to the sawbones.'

'Okay, so it'll take a week. Who's worryin'? Only Munroe. When he starts to enquire about us you'll tell him I met with an accident and will finish our deal when I'm better. Won't make no difference to him since he won't know what's coming.'

Lynch said no more. He had long ago discovered that it was no use arguing with Dyson once his mind was made up. But, deep down, Lynch was somewhat appalled by the immensity of Dyson's plan. To force a showdown by a shooting match and sweep Munroe out of existence was no little gamble. If it came off it would inevitably mean mastery of the whole town, but if it did not — Lynch gave a little shudder to himself and licked his lips.

'It might be a good idea,' Dyson said, 'if you went over to the gin palace when it opens and tell Munroe there'll be a delay because of my accident. At the same time weigh things up. See how many men we might have to deal with: try and figger out if any of 'em would be willing to play ball with us. Even buy their co-operation with greenbacks if you haveta.'

'Which means carryin' the whole thing to the size of a full scale revolt? I ain't sure I like that.'

'What you like doesn't matter: just do as yore told. Frum the look of the township a full scale revolt might give it the shake-up it needs.'

'Okay,' Lynch sighed — so that evening he did as he had been ordered and after explaining matters to the apparently sympathetic Munroe he spent the rest of his time trying to discover what kind of opposition there might be to a change of 'regime'.

The main thing he found out in his various conversations, was that Munroe was a square-shooter and much respected. It appeared that he had never pulled anything crooked in his life and, as a consequence, most of the people were solidly behind him. It seemed he also occupied the position of sheriff whilst his brother-in-law, a local well-to-do rancher, had been elected mayor. So even and undisturbed was the life of Mountain's End, however, no official power had ever been required. By and large, it appeared to Lynch, there could not be a town anywhere more unprepared for sudden violence and a switch in authority.

When he passed the information on to Dyson late that evening the outlaw grinned widely.

'Sounds like we'll have no more trouble with this than with a Sunday School picnic. Since there's never bin any trouble there won't be any experts with guns.'

'Nope — but there won't be anybody willing to side with us against Munroe,'

Lynch pointed out. 'I've made pretty sure uv that point.'

'Whatever the odds,' Dyson decided, 'we're goin' through with it. This durned leg uv mine is the only hold-up right now.'

But in the course of a week his tough constitution, to say nothing of his desperate desire to get a move on, had put him far enough on the road to recovery to enable him to move around with nothing more than a limp. This he disregarded since it did not hamper his movements to any great extent —

So the evening came when he made up his mind to go into action. His guns fully loaded and Lynch behind him, he entered the gin palace as casually as possible and wandered over to the bar where Munroe was standing chatting to a customer. Immediately he turned.

'Howdy, Mr Salter.' He held out his hand. 'Your pardner Mr Gregson was tellin' me you'd met with an accident. Glad t'see y' around again.'

'Thanks,' Dyson growled, and to the

barkeep he added, 'Make it gin.'

'On the house,' Munroe smiled. 'Or do I haveta tell you yore a lot more than just an ordinary customer.'

Dyson said nothing and, heavily bearded as he had now become, it was not possible to judge his expression. Only Lynch who knew him so well, could tell from the hard light in his eyes what was coming.

'I've bin doin' quite a lot of thinkin' about our deal while I've bin nursing my leg,' Dyson said, after a moment. 'The more I think of it the more it seems t'me I'd be a sucker to pay you fifty thousand dollars for it when there's another way.'

'Another way?' Munroe repeated, surprised. 'What other way?'

Dyson jerked his head. 'Have your lawyer come here and I'll show you. If he isn't handy, then get him.'

'Matter of fact he's right over there.' Munroe looked puzzled for a moment as Dyson downed his gin. 'Can't say I figger your angle on this, Mr Salter.'

Dyson said nothing. Lynch moved to a rear position behind him. Munroe gave a signal and a fat man in a black suit, his jacket bulging with papers and deeds, came waddling over.

'This is my lawyer, Mr Salter,' Munroe introduced. 'Albert Hindley — reliable a man as y'can find.'

'Good.' Suddenly Dyson's right-hand gun had flashed into his hand. 'Now just listen to this, gentlemen, and keep your hands down because I don't want t'attract attention. I've decided to take over this saloon without pay. I ain't botherin' about my legal right to it. This gun is my sayso.'

Munroe and the lawyer just stared, unable to swallow the audacity of the statement.

'If you don't know now, you will later,' Dyson continued, 'so I may as well tell you there's a price on my head. And on th' head uv my partner here. We're not cattlemen: we're outlaws. All we ever got we got with a gun, and I aim to go right on doin' it 'cos we've nothin' to lose. I've weighed up this town, and the people in it and there never was an easier snatch.'

'Yore absolutely crazy,' the lawyer said flatly. 'One man can't swing a deal when everybody is against it — and by that I mean the people around here. They wouldn't stand for it.'

'Right now they don't know anythin' about it,' Dyson retorted. 'Nor will they. The only two who can tell 'em anythin' are you and Munroe here, and if you value your lives you won't do that. Keep your voice down and do just as yore told. I wouldn't hesitate over rubbing either of you out 'cos I've done it with others and one more wouldn't make any difference.'

Munroe and Hindley glanced at each other. By this time it had dawned on them that Dyson meant business.

'To make it quieter we'll go to your office,' Dyson said, with a glance at Munroe. 'Hurry it up, and remember my pardner and I are right behind you.'

There was nothing the two men

could do but obey. Dyson leathered his gun for a moment but kept his hand on the butt. Not that this signified anything to the customers. They had not grasped the situation in the slightest. But once in the office with the door closed Dyson returned his gun to his hand and Lynch kept cover from the doorway.

'Well?' Munroe snapped. 'What the hell do you want to do?'

'I told yuh — take over. You, Hindley, draw up a deed right now which transfers this saloon to me. You can stick in the sum of fifty thousand dollars. That'll look legal frum my point of view even though no money is exchanged — '

'This is nothin' more than a damned hold-up!' Hindley blazed. 'It's as big a stick-up as robbin' a mail train — '

'Right,' Dyson acknowledged. 'That's exactly what it is, in a different sorta way. Give me credit fur having done a bit uv fancy thinkin' over this job. The way I worked it out is this: if y'can make a packet by holdin' up a train or a stagecoach y'can do it just the same with a saloon. An' once yuh've got the saloon yuh've got the centre of the town. Savvy? Now git busy on that deed, Hindley, and remember I'm watchin' you.'

'Do as he says,' Munroe ordered, as the lawyer hesitated. 'You can't argue with a six-gun. He'll never get away with it in the end.'

'Think not?' Dyson grinned through his beard. 'With that signed transfer in my possession nobody can shift me — not even all the law officers in Tucson.'

'Not as far as the deed is concerned perhaps,' Munroe admitted. 'Though I could prove that I never had payment. Forgetting that for the moment there's the fact that you've both admitted you're wanted men. The authorities would take you away on that account.'

'Providin' they ever get the facts,' Dyson said ambiguously. 'When I do a thing, Munroe, I do it properly. And,' he added, jabbing his gun in Hindley's fat back as he sat writing at the desk, 'don't try and put any funny clauses in that transfer. I know a thing or two about legal documents an' if there's any two-timing y'may not leave this office in one piece.'

The lawyer merely grunted and went on writing. Altogether it took him half an hour to pen the deed, which he finally handed to Munroe. At least he intended to do so but Dyson reached out and snatched it.

'Yeah,' he said finally, musing. 'Yeah, that's very pretty. An' there ain't no holes in it neither. Fur the sum of fifty thousand dollars this saloon and its stock-in-trade is transferred to me, Edgar Salter. That means — '

'It ain't legal,' Lynch put in briefly, and Dyson glanced at him.

'Why ain't it?'

'Cos your name ain't really Edgar Salter but Len Dyson.'

Dyson glared. 'Yuh big mug! D'yuh *haveta* open yuh mouth that wide!'

Lynch shrugged. 'Might as well put it

straight. Ain't no use havin' a thing in a name that ain't yuh own. Yuh'd have no right to th' property.'

'So *that's* who you are,' Hindley said slowly, his eyes narrowed. 'Len Dyson, huh? Then I figger your pardner here must be Lynch Corbett.'

'Check,' Lynch assented, undisturbed.

'You can expect no quarter from these hoodlums, Munroe,' the lawyer said bitterly. 'I happen to know from reward dodgers I've seen in Tucson and around that they're two of the worst outlaws in the territory. Hardly a thing that ain't pinned on them — murder, hold-ups, the works. I didn't recognise 'em with their beards. Just as well to know.'

'Stop talkin, pot-belly, and add an extra page stating that Edgar Salter is me, Len Dyson. I want this t'be legal.'

Hindley shrugged and wrote the addendum, initialled it, and then handed it back.

'Right!' Dyson examined it and then flung it on the desk. 'Sign both,

Munroe — and you witness it, Hindley.'

They did so, the cold muzzle of Dyson's gun not six inches from their faces. This done, Dyson added his own scrawl and then stood guard while Lynch added his own signature.

'Thanks,' Dyson said dryly, putting the deed in his pocket. 'Now, Munroe, you said you were due for a change of scenery. Start getting it. You've two hours to get outa town and take your wife and bag and baggage with you. An' remember, you'll be watched all the time. One word to anybody 'cept your wife — an' she don't matter since she'll go with you — I'll drop you in your tracks an' to hell with the consequences!'

Munroe tightened his lips but did not say anything. He began moving towards the door until Dyson stopped him.

'Wait a minute. Take this pot-bellied lawyer with you. The both of you can skip town together and don't come back — either of yuh. Now get out, and we're *still* right behind you.'

Both men left the office and walked silently through the crowded saloon. There was still nothing in their actions to arouse suspicion amongst the talking, drinking customers. Dyson kept close in the rear of the two men and Lynch followed at a slight distance, ready to draw instantly if need be. Until finally the quartet passed beyond the batwings to the boardwalk.

'How far do you two live?' Dyson asked briefly, and Munroe and the lawyer glanced over their shoulders.

'Two hundred yards down the street for me,' Hindley said.

'I'm at the Brown-S ranch,' Munroe added. 'About fifteen minutes' ride.'

'Okay.' Dyson gave Lynch a grim glance. 'You take pot-belly home, Lynch, and I'll do the same fur Munroe. They're not gettin' a chance to talk to anybody . . . ' Then with his voice at a whisper he added to Lynch: 'You know what t'do. We've gotta make ourselves safe with this lot.'

Lynch nodded but did not speak. He

moved to Hindley's side, jerked his head to him, and then accompanied him down the main street.

'All right, you,' Dyson snapped to Munroe. 'Git to your horse.'

Munroe went down the steps and untied his mare from the tie-rack. When he had mounted Dyson did likewise on his own horse and, Munroe leading the way, the pair went up the street. Once they were on the open, night-ridden trail beyond the town Dyson kept to the rear, ready for any sudden turn around with a gun which Munroe might attempt. However, he made no such endeavour — and finally, after about seven minutes of riding, Dyson called a sudden halt. He rode ahead to Munroe's side and drew rein.

'What's the idea?' Munroe asked, puzzled. 'We've quite a way to go yet.'

'No you ain't, Munroe. Far as yore concerned the trail ends right here. Yuh didn't suppose, once I'd gotten you to transfer the saloon t'me, that I'd be mug enough to let y'wander around and talk yuh head off, did yuh? You could make the whale uv a lot of trouble with the authorities — I'm rubbin' you out, Munroe, an' when yuh body's found, as it will be, the only clue'll be a forty-five slug in your carcase. Since most folks hereabouts use a forty-five there ain't a cat-in-hell's chance of me bein' suspect — '

Realising at last what was coming Munroe's hand dived to his gun, and never got there. Dyson fired three times with ruthless savagery and then sat watching as Munroe slowly slid from his startled horse and crashed into the dust of the trail.

After a moment or two Dyson grinned to himself; then he slapped Munroe's mare across the withers and sent it bounding in fright away up the trail. The night became silent again, with only Munroe's fallen body as evidence of the brief tragedy. Dyson stayed long enough to be sure Munroe was really dead, then he remounted and rode back into town.

He was tying his horse to the tie-rack outside the Naughty Lady when Lynch came gliding to him out of the shadows.

'Hindley's well taken care uv,' he murmured. 'How's about Munroe?'

'I finished him 'cos it wus the only safe thing to do. What did yuh do to Hindley?'

'Put a slug through him just as he was goin' up the path to his front door. I saw his old woman come out, then I quit. I figgered it weren't safe to stick around ... Y'know somethin', Len? The folks are bound to suspect us as th' culprits, partic'larly when they know we've taken over.'

Dyson spat. 'Let 'em suspect. They can't prove anythin'. Now let's get inter the saloon an' let 'em know who's boss around here frum now on.'

4

There did not appear to be any change amongst the customers of the Naughty Lady when Dyson and Lynch strode back into the main saloon-room. The cowpokes and their women were still there; the same batch of scroungers were still around the bar. Attention was only given when Dyson dragged up a chair, stood on it, then fired his gun overhead to silence the chatter.

'Fur the information of you folks there's been a change around here,' he announced, coming straight to the poimt. 'My name's Edgar Salter, and this is my partner Cliff Gregson. We're both cattlemen from up north. About an hour ago your much-respected friend, Mr Munroe, sold this saloon to me. Frum now on I'm boss around here and I'll do all I can to make you happy customers.'

Dyson paused for a moment at the

quick interchange of conversation, then:

'There'll be quite a few changes. Decorations and alterations are overdue and also there — '

He paused again and glanced towards the batwings as a distraught-looking woman with a kerchief thrown hastily over her grey head came hurrying in. She took one look towards the bearded Dyson then, ignoring him, turned to the people.

'I need help — quickly!' she shouted. 'There's some killer around here who's murdered my Albert! I heard a shot, and when I come outa the front door there he was in the path. Dead!' the woman finished hysterically. '*Dead!* Somebody put a bullet through his head.'

Immediately the men and women were on their feet, hurrying over to her as grief got the better of her. Dyson watched for a moment or two and then shouted above the voices:

'If there's a killer around here I reckon the only thing we can do is get the sheriff. Where is he?'

'Mebby *you* can tell us that,' one of the men said, grim suspicion in his grey eyes. 'Munroe's the sheriff, amongst other offices. What happened to him after you'd bought this property from him?'

'Far as I know he rode home,' Dyson shrugged. 'He told me he'd decided to quit town, so the sooner he got on the move the better.'

'Jake — ' The man with grey eyes jerked his head to a nearby cowpoke. 'Get on your way and fetch him. Tell him there's murder bin done.'

Jake nodded and swiftly departed. Dyson pushed his way through the crowd and then stood looking at the weeping woman seated on the chair.

'Anythin' I can do, ma'am?' he asked. 'I ain't got no legal authority an' I'm a stranger around here, but havin' become the owner of this saloon I've sort uv got some influence.'

The woman looked up slowly, her eyes still red from tears.

'I s'pose you'll be Edgar Salter, then?'

'That's right, ma'am.'

'Albert mentioned you were going to buy this place.'

'So far,' Dyson said, 'you haven't sed who Albert is — but I figger you must mean Albert Hindley, the lawyer.'

'Yes . . . ' The woman lowered her head again. 'An' there just ain't nothing you can do, Mr Salter. Ain't no power can bring the dead back, is there?'

Dyson shrugged and turned away, fully aware of the suspicion that still lay in the faces of the men and women. Not that he was disturbed. Suspicion was one thing, but proof was another . . . He eventually came up against Lynch as he lounged against the bar.

'Soft soap 'em,' Dyson murmured. 'One word the wrong way and we might have a shootin' match on our hands — specially when they hear that Munroe's bin wiped out as well.'

Presently the general tension was broken as a couple of the womenfolk came forward and led the grief-stricken wife of Hindley out of the saloon.

Dyson and Lynch watched her go, then they both tautened inwardly as several of the menfolk turned and came slowly back towards the bar. The foremost amongst them was the man with grey eyes who had made no attempt to conceal his suspicions from the very first.

'This whole set-up seems more than queer to me, Mr Salter,' he said bluntly, latching his thumbs in his belt as he stood arrogantly in front of Dyson. 'There's never bin any crime or trouble in this town worth mentionin' since it were built — yet the moment this property gets transferred the man who arranged it — lawyer Hindley — gets shot dead. Can't blame us fur thinkin' things, can you?'

'Just as long as it gets no further than that,' Dyson retorted.

'There ain't no call fur pitching into us,' Lynch growled. 'It's nothing but a coincidence. I reckon that a man like Hindley, being a lawyer, could very easily have plenty uv enemies. One of 'em must finally have gotten his own back.'

'There'd be nothin' to *get* back in the case of a man like Hindley!' The man with grey eyes stood his ground firmly. 'He was an honest lawyer and everybody liked him — Which is more'n I can say of you two gents,' he added sourly.

Dyson hesitated a moment then his fingers closed round the glass of gin on the bar counter beside him. Abruptly he flung the contents in his interrogator's face. In the same instant he whipped out his left-hand gun and held it steady.

'I'll stand so much,' Dyson said deliberately, as the grey-eyed man spluttered and wiped his face, 'but no more. I don't know who the hell you are — an' I don't durned well care — but yore not goin' to stand there and sling insults around. Savvy?'

The grey-eyed man clenched his fists and then looked about him on the others.

'You saw that, the whole bunch of

you! What are we goin' to do, anyways? Just stand for it?'

'Yes!' Dyson declared flatly. ''Cos I'm in my rights and 'cos I've got the gun. The rest of you folks would have good sense if yuh stopped listenin' to this trouble-maker. He don't know what he's talkin' about anyways!'

'Who don't?' the grey-eyed man snapped. 'I'll tell yuh right now what I'm thinkin' — that you an' your partner got this property by some trick or other and you polished off Hindley so he couldn't reveal anythin'!'

Dyson grinned crookedly. With his free hand he pulled out the deed of transfer keeping back the last page. Then he held it up whilst the men and women crowded around to read it. Their expressions showed that they were finally convinced, which they could hardly help but be with the whole thing set out in apparently perfectly legal order.

'Havin' read that, the lot of you, it's time yuh got somethin' straight,' Dyson said, returning the deed to his pocket. 'I'm the legal owner of this saloon and that being so I have the last say as to the type of people I'll put up with fur customers. All of you are welcome here as you were when Munroe owned it — but *you* can get out and stay out!'

The grey-eyed man glared. 'You can't tell me what to do, Salter!'

'I can — an' I am doin'! If I see you in here agen I'll have you thrown out. Or I'll do it myself — Now get out!'

'No — hold it a minnit.' Another man came forward. 'I guess that Dick Alroyd has always bin one for speakin' without thinkin', Mr Salter. Forget it if you can. He's a mighty useful person to all uv us, owning the general stores for one thing — and for another in this kind uv country yuh can't ban a man from having his drink. It's a necessity.'

Dyson slowly put his gun away and considered. Finally he gave a shrug.

'Okay, Alroyd. But mind what yuh say in future. I'll not stand insults frum you or anybody else — '

Dyson broke off and glanced up as a trail-dusty figure came in through the batwings. It was the cowpoke Jake who had been dispatched to find Munroe. Now he came forward, his face taut with excitement.

'Munroe's been shot too!' he exclaimed, reaching the bar and motioning for a drink.

For a moment there was an astounded silence. Dyson watched reaction narrowly and signalled for his own and the cowpoke's glasses to be filled.

'*Shot*, did yuh say?' Dick Alroyd came forward again, glad enough to seize upon a new opportunity. 'Where? When?'

'I found him on the trail 'bout a mile off, half-way to his spread. Weren't no sign of his mount.' Jake drank quickly. 'I found out he wus dead but I couldn't see what sorta damage had bin done to him so I brought him back with me. His body's on my cayuse outside.'

Instantly there was a general turn-about as the men and women crowded towards the batwings and then passed outside. Jake found himself left with Dyson on one side and Lynch on the other.

'Have another drink,' Dyson said, nodding to the barkeep. 'I guess you need it. Ain't anybody's idea uv fun to ride with a corpse for company.'

Jake nodded moodily and drew his sleeve over his face. 'I guess things like this ain't ever happened in Mountain's End before! Two killings in one night, and the victims both important men. We've lost the lawyer and the sheriff in one stroke . . . '

His voice tailed off as the men and women started to return, led as usual by the aggresive Dick Alroyd. Without pause he came up to the bar.

'I suppose *this* is coincidence too?' he sneered. 'I suppose it must ha' bin fairies that put three bullets into Munroe? One in the heart an' two in the head.'

'I've warned you already about insults,' Dyson snapped. 'I'm as surpised, and sorry, as you are to hear about

Munroe. He seemed to be one regular feller to me.'

'And I s'pose neither you nor this pardner of yourn know anything about it?' Alroyd demanded, resting his hands on his guns.

'Oh talk sense!' Dyson said irritably. 'It's obviously the work of some outlaw — some killer who's on the prod. Why he chose Hindley and Munroe we don't know, but I'd say in Munroe's case it must have bin because he was riding alone and wus an easy target.'

'Since Hindley and Munroe were rubbed out miles apart I'm sayin' two killers did the jobs,' Alroyd stated grimly. 'Mebby you dealt with one and your pardner with the other.'

'Now lissen, Alroyd — '

'You'll do the listenin' for a moment, Salter. We're a law-abidin' community here and we want things right. Give me both your guns.'

'What!' Dyson stared malevolently.

'You heard! I'm having the doc come over and dig one of the slugs out of

Munroe's body — and later mebby out of Hindley. If either of 'em match the slugs from one of your guns, or your partner's, the pair of you can look forward to a necktie party an' to hell with the authorities!'

Dyson smiled sourly. 'You take the hell of a lot for granted, Alroyd! If you'd asked me earlier for my guns I'd have let you have them — but not now. For some reason yuh've decided to make an enemy of me an' I'm sure not trustin' myself in front of you without my guns. I'm not that loco!'

'All right, since yore so leary, I'll have one gun at a time. That still leaves you one for cover — But I don't aim to shoot you. I only want to get at the facts.'

'On whose authority?' Lynch asked, surprisingly.

'I don't need no authority. I'm just — '

'Yore just makin' a damned nuisance uv yourself and nothin' more,' Lynch interrupted. 'I ain't sed much so far, but now I'm going ter. There's only one person, by law, who can demand a man's guns fur examination and that's the sheriff. Nobody else is entitled to.'

Silence and the men and women shifted slightly and then began nodding at each other.

'Yeah that's right enough,' somebody said. 'But in a case like this — '

'This case ain't no different frum any other,' Lynch snapped. 'You, Alroyd, have decided to pin everythin' on my partner and me for no apparent reason, and it's time you shut up. The only slugs you'll get from my partner's gun — or mine — will be in your belly unless you keep quiet . . . Get yourself a sheriff and then you can tell him what to do.'

'That's one sensible suggestion,' Dyson observed, 'even if we never git another.'

'How's about the mayor?' somebody asked. 'He's Munroe's brother-in-law and — '

'The mayor hasn't the authority of

the sheriff,' somebody else said. 'Since Munroe was sheriff we're now without one. Who's willing to stand fur nomination?'

'I am,' Dyson said calmly, and made the general amazement complete.

'You!' Alroyd exploded. 'You've got the damned gall to — '

'I'm merely standing fur nomination,' Dyson interrupted. 'I'm not sheriff' til I'm elected. And don't forget, any one of you who also wants the job, that a sheriff has got to be tough and level-headed. Which is more'n I can say for you, Alroyd.'

Alroyd swung angrily. 'Are we standin' for this?' he demanded. 'The possible killer of Munroe and maybe Hindley walks in and buys this place and then has the audacity to put himself up for sheriff.'

Alroyd did not get the roar of support he expected. Though in actual truth he had about the keenest mind of anybody and had already seen through the characters of the two bearded

119

'cattlemen from up north' the rest of the community were not so bright. It looked very much to them as though the impetuous Alroyd was seeking trouble for trouble's sake.

'Well, *well*?' Alroyd demanded. 'What the heck's the matter with you? You ain't standin' for it, are you?'

'I can't see so darned much wrong with it,' one man commented. 'Munroe was made sheriff because he was the most influential man in the town — The owner of the Naughty Lady is bound to be that. Also, running this saloon, it made Munroe able to keep an eye on every type in town. I can't see why Mr Salter shouldn't do the same.'

'But what if he's a killer?' Alroyd yelled.

'Take it easy,' Dyson snapped. 'You'll need a mite of proof before yuh start yellin' things like that. If you put me in as sheriff I'll still hand over my guns for proof — providing you keep this hothead Alroyd from shooting me down meanwhile.'

'You crazy?' Lynch whispered. 'The slugs'll — '

'Shut up,' Dyson growled. 'I know what I'm doin' — ' Then aloud:

'I've offered meself, but surely there's somebody else who wants to stand? It ain't just *me*?'

Nobody responded, though several men looked at each other. Dyson waited for a moment and then stepped forward and wandered in and out of the tight-packed assembly, calling for a second volunteer for sheriff. By the time he had finished his activities he had not only also tempted one other man into standing for nomination, but had also transferred his .45s in return. In the general press it had not been difficult — certainly not for a man as light-fingered as Dyson.

With a silent sigh of relief he returned to his former vantage point and held up his hand.

'That makes two willin' to stand,' he announced. 'Me, and that feller there, whatever his name is.'

'Jeff Roxburg,' said the nominee.

'Okay. Now it's up to you folks — Go an' git me a sheet of thick foolscap an' pen and ink,' Dyson added to Lynch. 'Whoever gets in we want it signed by a responsible majority. And,' he added in a whisper, 'there's two .45s hanging on that office wall. I noticed 'em when we wus in there. Get 'em in place of yourn.'

Lynch nodded and hurried off. Within a moment or two he was back. Dyson raised his hand again for silence, and it was accorded him. By this time even the belligerent Alroyd had become subdued and apparently willing to throw in his lot with the others. Whatever his personal suspicions there was no point to keep airing them unless he were given support.

'We'll decide this with a show of hands,' Dyson decided. 'It's quicker. All in favour of Jeff Roxburg for sheriff raise their hands — and you'd better count 'em, Alroyd, since yore so durned suspicious.'

There was a chuckle here and there at Alroyd's grim expression and Dyson felt he was beginning to enjoy himself. The folks were mainly with him, it seemed — more than a little tired of Alroyd's so far unfounded suspicions.

The hands rose. Dyson counted them for himself. There seemed to be an uncomfortably large number of them.

'Fifty-two,' Alroyd announced finally. 'You check that?'

The man on his right, counting for confirmation, nodded.

'Okay, fifty-two it is,' Dyson exclaimed. 'Now, how many for me? And count straight, Alroyd!'

The hands rose. Silently Dyson calculated, his eyes roving over the assembly. When he had finished counting he was smiling to himself.

'Sixty-one,' Alroyd growled. 'An' all I can say is you folks must be plain whacky.'

'Whacky nothin'!' came the retort. 'Jeff Roxburg ain't no use for sheriff. He ain't tough enough! If he saw an outlaw he'd probably hit the trail an' never come back.'

Jeff Roxburg grinned awkwardly amidst the guffaws, then he was spared further embarrassment as Dyson's voice boomed forth.

'Thanks fur the support, folks — '

'You ain't got my support!' Alroyd snapped. 'An' I reckon you never will have!'

'Okay, okay, so I'm short of one or two. That don't matter. A complete majority is unheard of, anyway. Those uv you who have voted fur me won't regret it. I'll serve you well — both as owner of the Naughty Lady, and as sheriff. One of you had best let the mayor know of the change in office. I don't know where to git hold of him. Only one thing missing — my badge. I didn't notice one on Munroe when I talked to him.'

'He carried it in his shirt pocket,' one of the men said. 'I guess it ought still to be there. I'll go look . . . '

'Seems to me there's more than *one*

thing missing,' Alroyd said grimly. 'What about the guns you were going to hand over? I ain't forgotten even if the rest uv the folks have.'

Dyson glared at him. 'You don't have to be so durned quick on the draw, do yuh? Let me get properly in office first.' He looked about him. 'Which uv you is any good at writing a document? I never could do that sort of stuff. I want it legal an' bindin' that I'm sheriff.'

A thin-faced man stepped forward. 'I guess I can do just that, I'm the editor of the *Mountain's End Gazette*.'

'Good enough.' Dyson handed over the foolscap. 'Get busy. Just put it nice and legal that I'm sheriff and represent the law.'

The thin-faced one hesitated as he took the paper. 'I can do that easily enough, Salter, but it won't be legally binding in itself.'

'Huh? Why won't it?'

'Because before it can become legal it's got to be counter-signed by the Tucson authorities. They won't raise any argument since all communities make their own elections — but the power vested in you isn't legal without their say-so.'

Dyson shrugged. 'All right, do what's necessary.'

'Right. After we've finished here you'd better come down to my office at the *Gazette* and I'll take a photo of you.'

Dyson started. 'Photo? What the hell for?'

The *Gazette* proprietor looked rather weary as he glanced up from writing at the table.

'For filin' of course. Every sheriff's photo is filed at the nearest authority headquarters. How else would they know who is the right dispenser of law for a certain district?'

Dyson hesitated and glanced at Lynch. Then he fingered his beard.

'Okay,' he said slowly. 'You know the rules. I don't.'

He said no more as the man who had gone to look for Munroe's badge was now pushing through the crowd with the badge in his hand. With a certain amount of solemnity he pinned it to Dyson's shirt.

'Good luck, Sheriff Salter,' he said, holding out his hand — and Dyson grinned to himself at the cheers — genuine and ironic — which came from all sides.

'Thanks a lot, folks,' he exclaimed. 'Now drinks for everybody — on the house. Includin' you Alroyd.'

'I'll drink — but I'll pay fur it,' Alroyd retorted. 'If it wasn't fur me wantin' to see justice done I'd turn me back on you right now. I'm still waitin' fur those guns uv yourn.'

'Time enough yet,' Dyson grinned. 'We need a drink first.'

And he deliberately kept Alroyd in suspense for a further half-hour. By this time the *Gazette* owner had completed the rough deed and obtained all the necessary signatures.

'I'll keep it to go with the photo for dispatch to Tucson,' he said.

Dyson nodded, then he inclined his head to one side as Lynch stood at his elbow.

'Yore not goin' to be such a sucker as t' let your photo go to Tucson, are yuh? It's askin' to be roped in!'

'With all this durned fungus around me face I can get away with anythin',' Len Dyson murmured. 'Anyways, I'm riskin' it. It'd look more'n a mite suspicious if I refused to have me picture taken. Ain't nothin' to worry over. I — '

He stopped as Alroyd's voice broke in: 'We're still waitin', Salter! Before somebody rides out to Munroe's ranch and breaks the news we want a few facts. An' we can start by examinin' your guns. One uv you go and fetch Doc Harrison.'

A cowpoke quickly departed; then Alroyd found himself considerably surprised as he saw that Dyson was holding his pair of .45s forward.

'All yours,' Dyson said calmly, and his eyes wandered to the man from whom he had appropriated the guns, substituting his own. He decided there was little chance of trouble. Both sets of guns were pearl-handled and both were .45s. The cowpoke would probably tell by the very feel of his own weapons that they were somehow different, but he hardly looked the type to pursue the matter to its logical conclusion.

'Something funny here,' Alroyd said, breaking the guns open. 'No shots ha' bin fired — but I distinctly remember you fired at the ceiling when you fust came in here tonight.'

'Sure I did,' Dyson acknowledged, thinking fast. 'Nothing to stop me reloadin', was there? Only an idiot doesn't reload to full capacity.'

Alroyd grunted something and shook the bullets from all the chambers into his palm — then he handed the guns back.

'Soon see if there's any sort of match-up,' he said. 'Just see to it, folks, that our new sheriff doesn't wander away until I come back. I'd better have

Doc Harrison take Munroe's body back to his own surgery — '

'Don't you want slugs from my guns too?' Lynch asked dryly, as Alroyd turned to go. 'Or have I suddenly become beyond suspicion?'

Alroyd grimaced and returned to where Lynch was holding his borrowed guns forward. Alroyd took out the bullets, made no comment, and then went on his way.

'I sorta get the feelin' that Alroyd is one mighty suspicious guy,' Dyson grinned, as the busily drinking customers closed around him again. 'I have the feelin' he and me are goin' to have trouble with each other afore we're through.'

'I reckon his bark's worse than his bite, sheriff,' one of the cowmen said. 'He always was a one for talkin' plenty was Alroyd.'

The conversation began to drift, but Dyson took good care to remain in the middle of it. It was essential to his newly-acquired position of sheriff and saloon owner that he make himself as popular as possible. Upon that groundwork he planned to build great things — aided by the gold creek several miles to the north. In fact, Dyson was feeling in great form and more than sure, in his present state of over-confidence, that nobody would ever find either him or Lynch tucked away in this remote Western township . . .

Then, presently, Alroyd returned. He was looking sombrely disgusted. Without a word he came to the bar counter and on to it tipped the bullets he had taken away.

'All yours,' he said briefly. 'Doc Harrison got a slug out and we checked it against these. Ain't even the same maker. So I guess that lets you out.'

Dyson raised an eyebrow. 'Thanks. Now perhaps yuh'll believe me in future when I say a thing is so — An' what about Hindley? Find anythin' concernin' him?'

Alroyd shrugged. 'No match on the slug. Whoever shot him and Munroe

131

certainly didn't use those guns uv yourn. In fact the slugs in both men are from different guns, so I just don't know where we stand. Up to you now, Salter.'

'Yeah?'

'As sheriff I mean. You'd better go to work to find who did the job. Community won't be satisfied until the killer's found. Way things are there ain't no tellin' when any uv us is safe.'

'I reckon there's a lot uv truth in that,' Lynch agreed sagely.

Then before Dyson could make any comment the *Gazette* man came forward. 'Better come down to my office, sheriff, and we'll get the picture taken.'

5

For Abe Jones life was commencing to pick up again, insofar as it could after the untimely and criminal decease of Sylvia. The first brutal shock of her death had subsided now and in its place had come an acceleration of the longing for revenge for the fate which had struck her down.

The funeral was finished with and two sobered parents were doing the only thing possible — carrying on with their normal lives and trying not to show the grief they felt. For Abe any attempt to lead a 'normal' life any more was out of the question. He was hell-bent on only one thing: the destruction of the two outlaws who had first robbed him and then killed Sylvia.

'I still insist that it's a job for the authorities,' old man Drew declared, when Abe talked it over with him. 'Now the funeral is over I'm free to move around. I'm riding to Tucson this very day. I'd like you to come with me, Abe, but if you prefer some wildcat scheme of your own that's somethin' I can do nothing about. But for God's sake don't go sticking your neck out in front of a couple of killers. If you do you'll finish up the same way as poor Sil.'

Abe clenched his fists. 'The moves the law will make are too unsatisfying for me, Mr Drew. When they find Dyson and Lynch they'll simply bring them in, try them, then hang them. And that's that. There's no personal satisfaction in it, no feeling that one had seen them smart, made them suffer — And I mean to *make* them suffer, if it's the last thing I do. A few months ago I'd have been scared to even look for 'em, but now — thanks to this bit of Courage Stone which dear Sil gave me — I'd tackle the Devil himself if I had to.'

'Yes.' Drew nodded soberly. 'Yes, I know exactly how you feel, Abe, and far be it from me to try and dissuade you.

Just the same the authorities have *got* to be told. You'd better come with me to Tucson and let's see how the land lies.'

Abe said no more. Within the next half-hour he and old man Drew were on their way. The journey was a long one, with its usual complement of blazing heat and arid dust. They talked little, both of them too filled with sombre thoughts — and beyond two stops at water holes they made the journey nonstop, arriving in Tucson in the mid-afternoon blaze.

Captain Derriker, head of the authorities and chief marshal for Tucson saw them immediately when they made their business known, and he listened in attentive, keen-eyed silence whilst the story of Sylvia's murder and the gold creek robbery was told.

'Which is just another way of saying that Dyson and Lynch Corbett are still running true to form,' Derriker said grimly. 'For the past few months we've lost track of them, even though we have rangers constantly on the look-out. You both have my very deepest sympathy for what's happened. Those two hoodlums are the scourge of the territory.'

'It isn't sympathy we want; it's action,' Abe said briefly. 'Apart from what's already happened, others are likely to fall foul of these outlaws. Sooner they're run-in, the better.'

Derriker reflected. 'Insofar as the gold creek is concerned there is no action we can take,' he said. 'There is no legal claim on it by you or anybody else, therefore it does not constitute a robbery. But in regard to the killing of your daughter, Mr Drew: that is a very different matter. Apart from the other crimes for which Lynch and Dyson are wanted, this further crime adds fuel to the fire. We shall have to redouble our energies to rope the men in for questioning.'

'*Questioning?*' Abe repeated, staring. 'But there's no doubt whatever about what they've done!'

'From your point of view I'm sure there isn't — and knowing those hoodlums as I do I'm quite sure you're justified. But we have the law to satisfy. We want absolute proof of this killing, and so far we have only your word for it, Mr Jones. You were the only one present when the murder took place. Lynch and Dyson could say — and indeed *would* say — that they did not commit the murder. Two of them against you. See what I mean?'

Abe clenched his fists. 'Look, I tell you — '

'I know. But the law always demands proof. There's no doubt that Lynch and Dyson will hang anyway for their other crimes, but in regard to this particular one, where you naturally want all the world to know the facts, you cannot pin the crime definitely without proof. That needs either another witness who saw the killing — a proof that Dyson's bullets caused the death of Miss Drew — or finally, a confession on his part made before witnesses. And those witnesses would have to be lawmen themselves. That's the situation.'

'Which is more or less what I

expected,' Tom Drew sighed. 'It isn't much consolation to see two men hang for a crime other than the one which we're interested in.'

For a while there was silence, Abe's brows knitted as he thought hard. Then presently an idea seemed to strike him and he looked up quickly.

'Tell me something, Captain — Is there any reason why I can't go after these two outlaws on my own account?'

'No reason at all — but I should add the warning that if you shoot them — and kill them — you'll be brought in and tried for it. Two wrongs don't make a right. Further, you'd have no legal authority for arresting them even if you located them.'

'Is there any reason why I can't have that authority? Can't I be appointed as a kind of unpaid marshal or ranger, drawing no salary, but having a roving commission — and above all the necessary authority for making an arrest if I want to?'

'Well now — ' Derriker drew a finger

slowly along his bottom lip, but before he could make any answer there was a knock on the office door and an orderly entered.

'Brought by special messenger from Mountain's End, sir,' he reported. 'It requires your special and immediate attention.'

'Thanks.' Derriker took the sealed envelope and the orderly departed.

'Mountain's End?' Abe repeated. 'That sort of strikes a note somewheres, Captain.'

'Indeed? Why?'

'I get most of my chow and general necessities from that remote township. I got to thinkin' recently that it might be the only possible town to which Lynch and Dyson could have got when they left the valley. Just a hunch.'

'Mmm . . . ' Derriker frowned at the envelope. ''Appointment of Sheriff',' he murmured. 'Must be a change of authority in Mountain's End. Pardon me a moment.'

He tore the envelope flap and then

139

extracted the photograph and detailed report from within. His eyes sharpened a little as he studied the bearded man in profile depicted in the print.

'Now I *wonder* . . . ' he mused — then he suddenly handed the photograph to Abe. 'Take a look at that. Resemble anybody you know?'

Abe looked and then gave a start. 'Hell's bells, it's him!' he ejaculated. 'The killer himself. Dyson!'

Derriker got up and went to the filing cabinet. When he came back to the desk he had a numbered print in his hand — a print of a clean-shaven man with hard jaws and a mouth like a steel trap.

'This is the print we have of Dyson,' he explained. 'But I guess there's no disguising the eye line, even in profile. Yes, it's Dyson all right, not very effectually disguised with a beard.'

'Manna from heaven,' old man Drew murmured. Then he frowned. 'Did you say something about appointment of sheriff?'

Derriker nodded. 'I did. This report

names Dyson as Edgar Salter, a cattle owner. It also states he has been elected sheriff of Mountain's End by general majority. Our job is simply to confirm the appointment by legal stamp and return it. When that's done the sheriff automatically assumes his mantle of office.'

'But — but how the devil did this killer ever get himself elected as sheriff?' Drew demanded blankly.

'I'm afraid that's one question I can't answer. The fact remains he *is* elected, and there's also no doubt of the fact that he's Dyson. We will confirm the appointment because we've no reason for not doing so — '

'But he's a wanted man!' Abe protested. 'Go and get him!'

Derriker smied a little. 'It isn't as easy as that. To the world this is Edgar Salter. Before we can lay a finger on him we have to prove he's Len Dyson. Don't think I enjoy the irritating demands of law, any more than you do — but I'm compelled to respect them

. . . However, all this gives me an idea, brings me back to your original notion of a roving commission, Mr Jones.'

'Yes?' Abe gave an eager glance.

'I'm going to swear you in as a marshal, specially assigned to this one case. I've done it before where a man happens to have exclusive knowledge of the job in hand, and you certainly have. On top of that you've good personal reasons for wanting to bring these hoodlums in. It might take our men months to get the information and facts that you can assimilate within hours . . . I'll give you a clear field, and the moment you want the full co-operation of the authorities you have only to notify me.'

'Suits me,' Abe said promptly.

'Very well. The swearing-in can begin right now — Excuse me while I get a witness.'

In ten minutes the job was done. Quietly Abe took the badge which was given him and slipped it in his shirt pocket.

'Now,' Derriker said. 'These are the only orders I am going to give you — Bring in Dyson and Lynch Corbett by any means you choose to adopt, but you must not harm either of them — not fatally that is. Also by any means you wish, you have to get proof of the fact that they murdered Sylvia Drew. Proof of their other crimes isn't necessary. We already have that. Also, before you can make any arrest, you have to show beyond doubt that these men — I include both of them, since Lynch Corbett has probably taken a different name — are using aliases. The rest is up to you.'

'I'll deal with it,' Abe said resolutely, getting to his feet. 'And thanks for giving me the opportunity.'

★ ★ ★

Abe's first move was to retire to the Bar-19 with old man Drew, which they reached towards midnight. Then, by the following morning, Abe had most of

143

the details of his plan worked out.

'I'll probably be away some time,' he told Drew and his wife, when he had come to the end of packing his horse for an indefinite trip. 'I'm going to keep on moving until I've put Dyson and Lynch where they belong. From time to time I'll keep you posted.'

More than this he would not say. He did not choose to give a hint of his plans, even to the entirely trustworthy rancher and his wife. One misplaced word might travel fast in the wrong direction and undo everything . . .

So Abe set off, and his first call was at the valley of the gold creek. He approached it with caution, even though he knew it was most unlikely anybody would be present. In this he was correct. Nothing disturbed the early morning peace. Quietly he rode down to the creek, dismounted, and tethered his horse to the post near the shack.

From the shack itself he brought out a panning-sieve — far simpler than searching for the old one which had

144

been thrown at him long ago. Thereafter, throughout the long day, he followed his former occupation of working at the creek — and apparently the luck was with him for the creek was giving up its bounty in no uncertain manner. Pan after pan of deposit contained the precious metal deposits.

One day passed — two days — three days. No disturbance, no anything, and Abe found himself the better off by two fairly large skin pouches of the precious metal, certainly ample for his immediate needs. One bag he put away in his belt for personal use; the other he tied to the saddle horn. After this he stayed only long enough to bar the shack and then rode on his way, arriving in the early afternoon at the desolate ruins of the old Redskin burial grounds where he and Sylvia had wandered together that long-gone afternoon.

As he stood gazing around him Abe seemed once again to feel her sweet presence near him. He fancied he could hear her voice, even her laughter. For a moment or two he was in a world of dreams, his eyes, somewhat moist, surveying the grim and eroded stones. Then with an effort he forced himself back to reality and went forward, descending finally into the tomblike region from where he had obtained his piece of Courage Stone.

Here again he had to fight the poignant power of memories. It was sheer hard work to keep his mind on his task. Deliberately he unfastened the bag of gold deposit which he had been carrying on his saddle horn — and then, quite promiscuously, he tossed the gold deposit in various directions until the bag was empty. The bag itself he pushed in one of the innumerable cracks in the walls.

'Yeah, I reckon that should do it,' he murmured — but as yet he had not come to the end of his activities. His next moves were to make certain rearrangements in the disposition of the huge boulders which lay against the walls. It took him an hour to get everything to his liking, then he quietly departed and came back into the blazing sunshine of the early afternoon.

'Best of luck, Sil,' he murmurd, removing his hat for a moment and staring into the cloudless cobalt of the sky. 'We'll meet again one day, and in the meantime I'll give those devils who snatched you away the worst time they've ever had on this earth.'

He returned his hat to his head and, grim-faced, went back to his horse. Amidst the solitary silence he ate some of the food he had packed, and then started on his way again, regardless of the afternoon heat. He timed his riding so that it was sunset when he came within sight of Mountain's End. Yet again he waited, having another meal, until at last the day had quietened into night and the icy winds of the mountains came sweeping down to dissipate the oven of the sunlit hours.

Abe rose, pulled on a mackinaw over his shirt, then hobbled his horse until he should need it again. He turned towards the light dots which had become Mountain's End and in the space of half-an-hour's sharp walking had reached the end of the main street.

Turning, Abe made his way past the rear of the buildings, thereby affording himself full concealment, until at length he reached the yard at the back of Alroyd's General Stores. His gentle tapping on the screen-door at last brought the store owner to open it. In some surprise he stared at his visitor in the light of the oil lamp hanging in the back porch.

'If it ain't Abe Jones!' Alroyd ejaculated. 'Yore sure ways past the ordinary shoppin' time, ain't you?'

'I've not come to buy anything, Mr Alroyd,' Abe explained. 'All I want is a word with you. Mind if I come in?'

'Sure, sure. More'n welcome.' Alroyd held the door wider and Abe stepped past him through the narrow corridor and into the neat oil-lighted living room.

'Howdy, ma'am,' Abe smiled at Mrs Alroyd — then Alroyd himself came in, looking vaguely wondering.

'Have a seat, Abe. What's this all about?'

'Well, actually it's pretty secretive.' Abe slid into a chair. 'I'm only telling you about it because in all the years I've dealt with you I know yore to be trusted — an' Mrs Alroyd too, of course.'

'Yeah — sure thing. Well?'

'I believe you've a new sheriff here?'

Alroyd's mouth set. 'That's right — Edgar Salter by name. An' there's some funny business connected with him only I can't quite make out what. He's got a partner by the name of Cliff Gregson. I did all I could to oppose his election as sheriff — Salter I mean — but I was beaten. I don't like the critter at all. Why do you ask? Fur that matter how do you even know?'

'I heard it from the authorities in Tucson. To cut a long story short, Mr Alroyd, I'm after this sheriff and his partner with everything I've got. They stole gold from me and murdered my girl. I guess that's reason enough.'

'Yeah, I guess it is,' Alroyd acknowledged then with a puzzled note in his voice he continued: 'Ain't none of my business, of course, but y'seem to have changed in some way. Yore not so much the Feather-Fist Jones I usta know.'

'No — and there's a reason for that. Anyways, to get down to cases. I want to know all there is to know about this sheriff and his partner. What more can you tell me?'

'Not much more, I reckon. It seems that Salter bought the Naughty Lady from Munroe, and Hindley drew up the deed. Next thing we knew was that Hindley and Munroe had both been murdered. No evidence to show who done it but I think it wus Salter and his partner. I insisted on checking their guns but I got no place. Hindley and Munroe were buried today and the murders have been reported to Tucson.'

'I see.' Abe considered for a moment. 'And I can promise you they won't do a thing about it.'

'Huh? Why not?' Alroyd demanded.

'What the devil's the use of the authorities if they won't do anythin'?'

For answer Abe pulled his marshal's badge from his shirt pocket and held it forward.

'A marshal? You?' Alroyd stared incredulously. 'Hell, but Feather-Fist Jones sure *has* changed.'

'I'm trusting both of you to say nothing about this. In fact I don't want anybody to ever know that I've been here at all. I've bin sworn in as a marshal for one purpose only — to bring in the sheriff and his partner, and that's what I aim to do . . . I need hardly add that their names are assumed. Actually they are two of the baddest hats in the territory — Len Dyson and Lynch Corbett.'

Alroyd stared. '*Them*! Come t'think on it I've seen reward dodgers up fur them up and down the trail! An' — an' is *that* who we've got fur sheriff and deputy?'

'That's it.' Abe gave a grim nod.

Alroyd got to his feet, his fists

clenched. 'Then it's goin' to stop right now! I'm goin' to the Naughty Lady an' tell the folks the facts!'

'No you're not,' Abe said quietly. 'You're not saying a word to anybody. That's the whole point. Like I just told you, my visit here is a secret. All I've done is give you the facts, but it's my job alone to deal with Dyson and Lynch.'

The impetuous Alroyd sat down again slowly. 'All right then: where do I fit into it?'

'Well, you know the people around here far better than I do. So who is there I can really trust? Somebody who looks like a grizzled pioneer and who can be relied upon not to give anything away concerning me?'

Alroyd rubbed his chin and stared ceilingward, then after a moment he snapped his fingers.

'I know — the very feller. Drygulch Henderson! He's around seventy and he's bin searchin' for gold in this territory since he was about twenty.

Always swearin' he'll find some some-day. I guess he can be relied upon — providin' you can keep him in liquor for a long time to come.'

'Won't be much difficulty about that,' Abe smiled. 'For that matter you could probably do with some liquor yourself, Mr Alroyd, in return for your trouble. Here . . . '

Abe tugged his gold-pouch from his belt and tipped some of the precious contents into Alroyd's horny palm. He stared at the gleaming dust and grit in amazement.

'I'll be durned if it ain't genuine gold! Where'd you get it? Struck a bonanza some place?'

'Could be,' Abe shrugged. 'How do you reckon I've kept goin' all these years without joinin' some ranch outfit? But forget that for the moment. Just accept that as payment for information — and for your silence. Now there's something else.'

'Sure, sure,' Alroyd agreed promptly.

'For obvious reasons I don't want to

be seen around. I'm laying a trap for Dyson and Lynch and this old-timer, Drygulch, will come into it. I want to talk to him. Think you can get him for me?'

'Can't think why not.' Alroyd glanced at the clock. 'I guess he'll be at the Naughty Lady. Never known him to miss a night yet. When I've got him what do I do with him?'

'Bring him to me at the back of your yard outside. I want our talk to be private — Not that I don't trust both of you,' Abe added hastily, 'but I think the old-timer will respond better if he doesn't have a third party in on it.'

'Okay. Let's go.'

Alroyd snatched down his hat and led the way outside. Then he went on his way into the darkness whilst Abe lounged around and waited, considering the light reflections from the kerosene lamps of the high street. After an interval of perhaps ten minutes there were footsteps and Alroyd came dimly back into view, accompanied by a short, wiry man, his face vaguely visible as masked in grey stubble.

'Up to you,' Alroyd said. 'Come agen some time, Abe. Always welcome.'

'Thanks a lot, Mr Alroyd.'

Abe waited until the screen door had shut behind the dealer and then he turned.

'You're Drygulch Henderson, I suppose?'

'Yep, sure am. But I ain't a-goin' ter say I know what all this is about, 'cos I don't. No, sir!' And Henderson spat emphatically.

'I'll soon wise you up. Before I start doin' it I'd better tell you that Alroyd says you're fully to be trusted, no matter what. That you're a square shooter.'

'Sure am.' There was the drifting stench of chewed garlic. 'Man an' boy I've bin around these parts an' y'can ask anybody yuh like what they think uv Drygulch. Yuh'll always git the same answer — square shooter. Yes, sir!' And more expectoration.

'That's good enough for me,' Abe

murmured. 'Now look — I hear you've been prospectin' all your life and never hit a bonanza.'

'That's right, but I ain't given up hope yet. No, sir.'

'That's just as well, because you *have* found a bonanza, and I want you to make that fact known to just two people — Sheriff Salter and that deputy of his. I forget his name.'

'I know 'em, but — Look, what the heck *is* this? I found a *bonanza*? I ain't even come within smellin' distance uv one yit. No, sir!'

'That's where you're wrong. A bonanza exists at the ancient ruins of a Redskin mausoleum. I don't suppose you'll know where it so so I'd better draw a map — '

'Don't know where it *is*!' Drygulch echoed. 'I sure do! It's some miles to the north of here. I've bin through it many a time. But it ain't no bonanza. I've toothcombed it, I reckon.'

'Then you missed something,' Abe said calmly. 'Here — take a look at this.

Hold out your hand.'

Drygulch obeyed and his thin, wiry body tensed as gold grit poured into his palm. He peered at the deposit in the starlight; then finally he struck a tinder down his pants with his free hand and looked again in the guttering flame.

'Durn me if it ain't gold!' he ejaculated, and dropped the tinder in his amazement.

'From the Redskin mausoleum,' Abe said deliberately. 'You can have that gold dust for yourself, Drygulch, and there'll be plenty more if you do exactly as you're told. I'm goin' to be quite frank with you and tell you what I'm driving at, but I'm relyin' on you never to tell anybody else, and most certainly not the sheriff and his deputy. I'm a marshal . . .'

Abe pulled out his badge and exhibited it in the starlight.

'Yeah, so I see. So what?'

'I've been specially commissioned by the Tucson authorities to get the sheriff and his deputy. They're both a couple of dead wrong 'uns.'

'They are, huh?' Drygulch spat again. 'I always figgered there was somethin' about 'em I didn't like, but it ain't none of my business.'

'It is now because you're the chief decoy . . . As I said, I want you to let them know, by any means you care to adopt, that you have struck a rich bonanza at the old Redskin mausoleum. Make sure they know its situation and all about it.'

'That won't be difficult — but where's the point when there ain't no bonanza there?'

'But there *is*. Leastways, there's enough gold scattered around to make it look the real thing, and unless I'm mistaken our two crooked friends will start pulling the place to bits to try and find the rest. That doesn't concern you, Drygulch. Just do as yore asked.'

The old prospector hesitated, scratching his nose. 'An' you say there's gold a-lyin' around for the pickin' up at the mausoleum?'

'Yes — but it's only put there as bait, *not* for you to go and start picking it up. Whatever gold you want I'll give you, but I'm relyin' on your honesty to stay away from the mausoleum. That's why I had Alroyd find me an honest man.'

Drygulch sighed. 'I get it — but you sure are throwin' a lot uv temptation in me way. Right! So I let the sheriff and his deputy know. Then what do I do?'

'Tell me their reactions. You'll find me just half-a-mile or so beyond the northern end of the main street. I've got my horse there waitin' for me, but I'm not moving on until I know how you've got on. Nothin' to stop you getting busy tonight, is there?'

'Nope, I reckon not. An' when I've reported do I git more gold?'

'I guess so. You'll be rewarded well enough.'

'Okay, see you later . . . ' And with his queer, shambling walk Drygulch Henderson went on his way. Abe watched him go, reflected on the wisdom of his actions, and then decided he had no other course. He turned away too and went silently into the darkness . . .

Meantime Drygulch reached the Naughty Lady. When he got up the steps to the batwings he paused for a moment, loosened up his shoulders, and then ambled into the saloon with the lurching gait of a man supremely drunk. The fatuous grin he managed to add to his wizened face heightened the effect.

'Howdy, Drygulch,' somebody called. 'Yuh sure got yuhself a bellyful, ain't you?'

'Sure did,' the old-timer agreed. 'Mebby yuh'd do the same if yuh felt like I do . . . ' He burst abruptly into song, reeled to a nearby table, and dropped heavily in the chair beside it. Then at the top of his voice he yelled: 'Whisky! An' make it quick!'

The barkeep hesitated and gave an inquiring glance at Dyson.

'What do I do, Mr Salter? Looks to me as though Drygulch has had as much liquor as he can hold already without more. He might start makin' trouble.'

'More than probable,' Dyson agreed. 'Leave him be — And who is he anyways? Looks like a saddle-tramp.'

'Quite one of the regulars. Bin comin' for years. Drygulch Henderson by name. Spends his time prospectin' fur gold that he never finds — Mystery is how he manages to make a livin' at all.'

'Lookee here!' Drygulch himself had come up, his whiskery jaw projecting aggressively. 'Where's that whisky I ordered? How long d'yuh haveta keep a man waitin'?'

'Don't you think you've had more'n enough, old-timer?' Dyson asked, and the old prospector squinted at him.

'Who the heck are you t'tell me what to do?'

'Me? I'm Edgar Slater, the proprietor of this saloon, and if I think you've had enough I'll say so. Best thing you can do is git into the night air an' cool off.'

'Now listen!' Drygulch slapped his

palm on the counter. 'When I say I want whisky I mean it — Think I can't pay fur it, I suppose? Well I can, y'know. Yes, *sir*!' And a small gold nugget bounced onto the counter beneath the barkeep's popping eyes. Both Dyson and Lynch saw it and exchanged quick glances.

'Bin a long time, I reckon, since anybody paid fur their drink in gold,' the barkeep observed, testing the fragment between his teeth. 'What do I do, *boss*?'

'Give him as much drink as that nugget's worth,' Dyson said; then with a genial grin he clapped the old-timer on the shoulder. 'I wasn't holdin' out on you, Drygulch. Just playin' games, that's all. From the looks of that gold you struck it lucky some place, huh?'

'Yeah, but I ain't sayin' where, so don't ask me!'

With a black-toothed grin Drygulch picked up a glass of whisky in each hand and pursued an unsteady course to the table in the corner. Once there he plumped down to enjoy himself.

'D'you suppose he's been monkeyin' around that gold creek?' Lynch asked suspiciously, watching him.

'I wus just wonderin' about that myself. We'd better find out — an' if it isn't the gold creek, then he's got a bonanza some place else. Might be useful to us. Save us goin' to the creek and takin' a risk every time we want gold.'

On that, Dyson strolled leisurely forward and settled at the table. Drygulch eyed him suspiciously.

'Well, what in heck d'you want now?' he asked belligerently. 'Can't a man even drink in peace?'

'Sure, sure,' Dyson responded soothingly. 'Go right ahead. When you're finished we just want a talk with yuh.'

Drygulch said nothing, but his eyes narrowed suspiciously. He was commencing to wonder if, in volunteering to carry out this project, he had not perhaps put himself in considerable danger. There was something in the expressions of both men that he did not quite like. He became even more sure of approaching trouble when, at the end of his drinking, Dyson got up and hauled him to his feet by the back of his shirt collar.

'Now, old-timer, outside,' he murmured. 'And be quick about it!'

There were guffaws and yells as the old prospector was bundled towards the batwings, with the broadly grinning Lynch following up in the rear. The chucking out of an intoxicated man from the Naughty Lady was nothing new — and certainly nobody save Dyson and Lynch knew the objective behind it. This became clear when they had at last half-thrown the swearing Drygulch down the boardwalk steps and into the main street.

'Sorry to treat yuh rough,' Dyson apologised dryly, as he jerked Drygulch on to his feet. 'Just one of those things that's necessary now an' agen. 'Sides, we wanted yuh out here so's we can deal with you without everybody watching an' listening.'

'Watchin' an' listenin' about what?' Drygulch demanded, trying to tear free — and failing.

'That gold uv yourn, of course. Where'd you get it frum?'

'Ain't no business of yours!'

'I kinda reckon it is.' And regardless of the man's age and much lesser figure Dyson lashed out his right with all his power. It sent Drygulch spinning and dropped him on his face in the dust.

'See what I mean?' Dyson asked, coming over to him. 'Git started talking, yuh dirty saddle tramp! Quick!' And he delivered a kick in the old-timer's ribs which brought him up struggling as far as his knees.

'Just how much yuh get beaten up depends on how fast yuh talk,' Lynch added grimly. 'We mean business, old-timer. Gold, like as you throw around, is too good fur a hombre like you! Where'd you *get* it?'

'All right, all right,' Drygulch gasped, struggling up and rubbing at his blood-streaked nose. 'I ain't aimin' to git smashed up just yet. I'll tell yuh ... There's a bonanza at the Red Indian mausoleum a coupla miles to the north.'

Dyson frowned. 'What kind uv line are yuh tryin' to pull? I've seen that mausoleum many a time — even been through it — but I ain't never seen any gold there.'

'Neither did I until recently. Must ha' bin some kind uv slip in the walls or somethin'. Anyways, there's gold fur the pickin' up.'

Dyson considered for a moment and then he grinned. 'Well, I reckon that's worth knowin' anyways — an' right now yore figgerin' how quickly you can git there before my pardner an' I do, huh? You can spare yuhself that bit of brainwork, old-timer. You ain't goin' no place — no more — '

'No?' With a suddenness which was startling for a 'drunken' man Drygulch whipped both his guns into his hands and levelled them. 'I'm a sight older than you, an' a durned sight more experienced,' he said, and spat forcibly. 'Take more'n a coupla critters like you to git the better uv me. You've forced it outa me where the gold is, but you ain't gettin' no further than that. No, sir! I'm on me way — and to hell with the both of yuh.'

With that he slowly retreated, keeping his guns at the ready; then when he had come to one of the narrow alleyways between buildings he dodged abruptly out of sight.

6

'Hold it!' Dyson ordered, as Lynch whipped out his gun and was about to hurry forward. 'Let the old fool go. If there's any firin' goes on we'll bring the whole populace out to see what it's about. Some of 'em are suspicious enough as it is without starting more trouble.'

Lynch scowled, releathered his .45, and came back to where Dyson was standing.

'All very well in its way,' he said, 'but there's nothing to prevent that old devil ridin' straight to the mausoleum and cleaning up all the gold he can find — before we can even git a hand on it.'

'Yeah, I guess that's possible,' Dyson admitted. 'But he won't get there fast since he doesn't seem to have a cayuse. Leastways, he didn't have it outside the saloon. Best thing you can do, Lynch, is get your horse an' go an' deal with him.

Y'know what direction he'll take if he heads fur the Redskin mausoleum.'

'Okay, I'll be on my way.'

'And when you've rubbed him out come straight back,' Dyson added. 'We sure ain't agoin' to any mausoleum just yet — neither uv us.'

Lynch paused and turned in surprise. 'Why not? If there's gold fur the pickin' up we — '

'It can stay until we're ready. Drygulch and us is the only ones that knows about it — fur as we can tell — so with him outa the way we'll do it in our own good time.'

'Can't think why we haveta wait. Gold has a mighty strong pull.'

'I know — but so has this town we've taken over. If either uv us — or both uv us — was away fur any length of time, as we well might be in hunting a bonanza, we'd find ourselves pushed out by those in the town who don't want us. I'm not riskin' that. We can only hold what we've got by stayin' right here an' leaving the gold for a convenient moment. There's a big build-up waitin' for this town an' no bonanza is goin' to throw me off it. Now yuh'd best git on your way and deal with Drygulch afore he gets too far. I'm goin' back into the Naughty Lady.'

Lynch nodded and headed for the tie-rack whilst Dyson went swiftly up the boardwalk steps. Neither of them was aware that the old and wily Drygulch Henderson had heard every word they had said. He had not been exaggerating when he had said he knew all the tricks: right now he was lounging in one of the nearby alleyways, crouching forward as much as he dared, his jaws moving ceaselessly over a wad of garlic. For the past few minutes the still air of the night had carried the words of Dyson and Lynch plainly to him since he had taken good care to remain down-wind from them.

'Wise guys,' he commented to himself, and ejected a stream of yellow juice into the dust — then when the two gunhawks had parted he turned swiftly and headed to the spot where he invariably left his horse — tied to a post at the rear of the saloon, an old gag so that no cowpoke could suddenly yield to the impulse of stealing the bright little pinto. Contrary to belief, Drygulch did not peregrinate on foot. He knew too well the rigours of the territory.

'Looks like we got some trigger-happy mugs in charge of things around here, Slinky,' he told the animal, climbing nimbly into the saddle. 'Mebby we'd best go an' tell the marshal what goes on. I sure hope that deputy sheriff enjoys himself lookin' fur me.'

With a grin he jolted the swift little animal into action and thereafter he took a wide detour which he knew would mean 'deputy sheriff' Lynch Corbett could never find him. Eventually he came riding up to the point where Abe Jones had said he would be waiting. He was. He came quickly out of the starlight as Drygulch came in view.

'Well?' Abe asked quickly. 'Did you do as I asked?'

'Yeah, I sure did — an' nearly got me brains beaten out doin' it. Yes, sir! Anyways, I reckon it didn't work.'

'Didn't work?' Abe repeated, disappointed.

'Not in the way you expected, that is. Those two crooked hyenas didn't dash straight off to the Redskin mausoleum like you figgered they would. No, sir! They decided to let it wait until they were good an' ready to go.'

'You mean they didn't believe you?'

'Shucks, no! They believed it all right, but they talked it over in the street after they thought they'd gotten rid uv me, an' far as I could figger out they reckoned they'd too many things to do right in Mountain's End to start movin' off after a bonanza. They also reckoned that I wus the only one knowin' about it outside themselves so the deputy sheriff set off to rub me out somewhere on the way to the mausoleum.' Drygulch spat easily. 'He's sure goin' to have one helluva search.'

'Yeah, I guess so,' Abe acknowledged,

musing. Then: 'The real answer to all this, as I see it, is that those two hoodlums don't mean leaving town in case they lose their grip on it. That seems to indicate that there must be a pretty strong opposition that they're afraid of.'

'Sure is,' Drygulch confirmed. 'Them two carrion-crows ain't sittin' pretty by any means. No, sir!'

'How d'you mean?'

'I'm just speakin' from experience, that's all. Frum what I've heard in the Naughty Lady it's only just beginnin' to dawn on a lot of 'em that these two gunhawks have held the town to ransom. Somehow they've gotten themselves into a position of influence an' it's more than plain that before long they'll stretch out further and take whatever they want. I reckon they'll get thrown out, or filled with lead, the moment the opposition to 'em becomes bigger than the support.'

'In which case,' Abe said, 'the only thing to do is get some organisation into the opposition. Once cleared out of town these hoodlums would make straight for the mausoleum — and that's what I'm aimin' at. Okay, Drygulch, that's all. You've done a good job.'

'Think nothin' of it.' Pause. 'An' I'm still not to go to the mausoleum an' pick up whatever I can find?'

'Under no circumstances! You're pledged to stay away from it — But here's some more gold as compensation.' Abe shook it into the waiting palm. 'All you've got to do now is get going and keep out of the territory.'

'I guess I don't need any encouragement to do that. That deputy sheriff will have a bead on me frum now on — so the further I git away from here the better. Lookee here, marshal, what difference will it make to your plans when that deputy can't find me? He'll figger that I might go to the mausoleum any time, an' that might set him and the sheriff himself headin' for the mausoleum bonanza after all.'

'You can let me worry about that,' Abe said. 'Just get on your way — an' thanks.'

Drygulch shrugged and said no more. Abe stood for some time pondering after the old prospector had vanished — then, finally making up his mind, he walked back towards the town and finished up once more at the rear of Alroyd's general store. As before it was Alroyd who opened the door, holding an oil lamp above his head.

'Oh, you again, Abe! Come right in.'

Abe followed him into the cosy living-room and both Alroyd and his wife gave questioning glances.

'Well, how'd you make out?' Alroyd questioned. 'I didn't go to the Naughty Lady tonight as I usually do in case I started talking too much. Y'know me! I sort of say too much sometimes — 'specially after a drink or two.'

'I partly made out — partly not.' Abe put down his hat and dragged up a chair. 'I think I'm goin' to have to call on you for help, Mr Alroyd.'

'Okay with me. I'll do anything I can.'

'Good. Well, the lay-out at present is that neither Lynch nor Dyson are likely to fall for the trap I've set them unless they find Mountain's End is too hot to hold 'em. As things are right now even gold isn't sufficient bait to drag 'em away!'

Alroyd gave a grim smile. 'That's only another way of sayin' that they're leary of leaving for any length of time in case they find certain factions have moved in on 'em.'

'That's it exactly. So before they start to extend their activities and gain a tighter hold they've got to be dislodged — while they know the bait of gold is still fresh. That's where you come in. I want you to stir up the opposition into a solid fighting force.'

'That shouldn't be difficult. There's dozens who'll willingly work against those two gunmen 'most any time you like.'

Abe's face became serious. 'The time

I'd like is now, Mr Alroyd. I want to get things moving by tomorrow night.'

'*So* soon?' Alroyd looked dubious.

'Yes — while the bait's still fresh, as I said before. By tomorrow evening, using whatever means you care to adopt, I want a solid army of men and women ready to shoot it out with Dyson, Lynch, and whatever gang they have on their side. It's bound to be rough going but they've got to be licked. The moment they realise that they are they'll hot-foot it for where they know gold is. Leastways, that's how I figger it.'

Alroyd considered. 'Am I supposed to know where this gold bait is, or isn't that in the programme?'

Abe smiled. 'You said yourself you talk a bit too much sometimes, especially after a drink. I'd rather not take that chance. A word in the wrong place might send a horde after that supposed bonanza and wreck my arrangements.'

'Okay, I respect your viewpoint. So

I'm to organise a mob to shoot it out. An' what'll you be doin'? Far as I can remember you ain't much good in a fight, didn't you say?'

'That's in the past,' Abe answered quietly. 'Sylvia Drew gave me something which destroyed the timidity I used to have. I shall be very much to the fore in this lot because I'm the one who's goin' to touch off the powder-keg.'

Alroyd nodded, even though he looked vaguely surprised.

'About mid-evening tomorrow,' Abe continued, 'I'll walk into the Naughty Lady and start things moving. The very fact of my walkin' in will start something, since that's about the last thing either Dyson or Lynch expect. You'll see for yourself when things are reaching flashpoint. The moment that happens your men must be ready to support me . . . Come to think of it, I sed men and *women*. Better leave the women out. There'll be plenty of rough stuff in this lot. Wherever you can dissuade women customers from going to the Naughty Lady tomorrow night, do so. Well, that's the lay-out. Think you can handle it?'

'I reckon so.' Alroyd glanced at the clock. 'If it comes to that I can start a few things movin' tonight. Leave it at that, then — and I'll see you tomorrow.'

Abe nodded, got to his feet, and picked up his hat. Adding a few further details, he accompanied Alroyd to the door.

★   ★   ★

Some time in the early hours Abe returned to the Bar-19 and, as he had expected, found it in darkness. Without making any sounds he forced the window of what had formerly been his bedroom, crept inside, and thereafter comfortably passed the night. The astonishment of old man Drew and his wife was complete when they beheld Abe arriving, freshly shaved, at the breakfast table.

'I don't think any apologies are necessary,' Abe smiled. 'I didn't want to wake you up and my old room seemed the best place to sleep on my journey to Tucson. That's where I'm heading this morning.'

'To see Captain Derriker?' Drew hazarded.

'Right. I've got things more or less lined up for a showdown and Derriker's the man who's got to know what's happening . . . ' And over the ham and eggs Abe added an explanation of his recent activities.

'So now your idea is what?' Drew enquired.

'I'm hoping that those skunks will fall for the bait I've laid and head for the mausoleum in the hope of finding a bonanza — '

'Why should they?' Drew asked slowly, thinking. 'They already know they can find gold at the valley creek.'

'True — but that sort of gold takes quite a time to get, and it's by no means reliable. Gold only appears every now and again. On the other hand, at the bonanza at the mausoleum — far as they know — they have gold for the picking up. That's definitely where they'll go. Anyways, I'm going to gamble on it. If that happens, Derriker's men can do the rest.'

Abe had little more to say than this: he was too busy with his own thoughts. Then the moment breakfast was over he started on the long journey to Tucson with the final statement that he had no idea when he would return. He was prepared for, and underwent, a gruelling journey — insofar that when he had reached Tucson and discussed matters with Derriker, he had only time for a brief rest before making the return trip on a borrowed horse. By and large, the day had punished him pretty considerably when he was again riding within the vicinity of Mountain's End — but at last he had the satisfaction of knowing that matters were planned to the last detail as far as he was concerned.

Within the Naughty Lady Dyson and Lynch were present as usual — the one covering the other surreptitiously, also as usual — in case of trouble. Lynch for his part was more than concerned that in spite of long riding and searching, both during the night and the day, he had not once spotted any sign of Drygulch Henderson. The one thing he had done had been to go as far as the mausoleum itself and satisfy himself that the bonanza existed. To all intents and purposes it did and he was privately the richer by a good deal of gold dust and small nuggets. At least he had had the brains not to take all the eggs out of the basket. But Drygulch Henderson was somewhere abroad. He might choose at any time to clean up the bonanza. Then what? Altogether, Lynch was taking a dim view of Dyson's resolution to stick in Mountain's End and gain control over it when there was gold for the picking up not very far away.

And it was upon this point that Abe walked into the saloon — calmly, not even with his hands on his guns. Without a word he crossed over to the bar. One or two customers glanced, but nothing more. A stranger passing through Mountain's End was no novelty. Naturally, the most prolonged stares came from Lynch and Dyson. From their different positions they gazed fixedly, just as though they could not believe their own eyes.

'Rye,' Abe said briefly to the barkeep, then when it had been served him he glanced around. In that one brief look he observed the fact that Alroyd was there, and the very faint inclination he gave to his head was sufficient indication that he evidently had everything under control. Also in his glance about him Abe encompassed Dyson and Lynch. Despite their beards he picked them out in a moment. He found himself wondering how they would react. If they recognised him publicly it would destroy their false identities as Salter and Gregson.

Then Dyson seemed to make up his mind. He came forward slowly.

'Stranger around here, mister?' he

asked, and it sounded as if he were endeavouring to be affable. 'I'm Salter, new owner of this place, and I'm not too familiar with the customers as yet.'

'They call me Feather-Fist Jones,' Abe replied calmly. 'And your name isn't Salter. It's Len Dyson, the monicker of one of the biggest outlaws in the territory. Don't try and fool me with that fancy beard!'

Abe spoke so loudly that those assembled could not fail to hear him. Men glanced up and listened intently. Lynch began to drift gradually into a position where he could fire without hurting anybody in the process of getting his target.

'Them's pretty dangerous words, mister,' Dyson said grimly. 'I reckon yore mistaken' me for somebody else.'

'No.' Abe shook his head. 'If I had a razor handy I'd shear off that mesquite bush you've sprouted an' let all the folks here see that your face is on reward dodgers the length and breadth of the territory.'

Suddenly Lynch's gun flashed up. At

the same instant it went hurtling out of his hand to the explosion of Abe's own gun. There followed a breathless pause.

'Don't think I didn't see you, Lynch,' Abe said deliberately. 'And don't get any fancy ideas about shootin' me up. I've got you taped: the both of you.'

Abe glanced briefly sideways as he spoke, and a second later he realised what a mistake he made. It was the one chance Dyson was waiting for. His right slammed out and struck Abe under the jaw, sending him sprawling in the sawdust, his gun sailing out of his hand. Instantly Lynch darted across and grabbed it.

'Get up!' Dyson snapped. 'An' be quick about it.'

Abe obeyed slowly, knowing that his life was in considerable danger. On one side of him, ranged against the counter and ready for any action Dyson decided to call upon, were the elements who had evidently decided to support their crooked 'sheriff'. On the other side amongst the tables, doing nothing as yet, were Alroyd and the grim-faced men that he had drawn unto his own banner. As far as Abe could tell, in the brief glance he gave, the two sides were roughly equal.

'Well, Mr Feather-Fist Jones, what now?' Dyson asked, grinning through his beard. 'Any more insults and false accusations to sling around?'

'Plenty,' Abe responded, apparently calm. 'I'm accusing you of hold-ups and murder — particularly the murder of one Sylvia Drew. You killed her way back in a gold-creek valley and she just didn't stand a chance. I reckon it's time these good folks knew about it. I don't think they'll take to the idea of a killer as their sheriff. And this deputy of yours — Lynch Corbett to give his right name — isn't much better.'

'This true, Salter?' Alroyd demanded, moving forward — and Dyson gave him a glance.

'You shut up, Alroyd. You always did talk too much. True? Course it ain't true! This Lilywhite has just drifted in with a lot of fancy tales. My partner and I met him way back — before we arrived here — and even then he was calling us all the names he could think of, for no partic'lar reason. We beat him up for his trouble and he didn't have the nerve to fight back. Plain yellow is this critter. As for this gal he talks about, I never even heard of her.'

'He doesn't seem so yellow to me,' Alroyd said — and Dyson glared at him.

'I thought I told you to shut up?'

'Can't think why I should. There's the hell uv a lot of things that are too one-sided. The way you duped most of these folks into votin' you in as sheriff fur one thing, and — '

Abe leapt. For a split second Dyson had relaxed his attention to look at Alroyd — the very thing Alroyd had been working for. Dyson found his gun-wrist gripped and twisted backwards with savage force. The sudden pain brought tears to his eyes and his gun dropped. He wheeled in fury — to meet a ramrod fist straight in the face.

Swearing, he tumbled backwards and clutched frantically at the edge of the bar counter to save himself falling.

'The main issues can wait for the moment,' Abe said, advancing on him. 'Right now I'm going to disprove one thing to the satisfaction of all these people: I'm going to prove that yore a damned liar in calling me yellow.'

'Why, you — ' Dyson catapulted himself forward from the bar without troubling to finish his sentence. At the same instant his left fist whipped up a haymaker which would probably have cracked Abe's jaw had it landed.

It didn't. Instead Abe dodged nimbly and hooked out his foot. Dyson couldn't help himself falling over it and he landed with a metallic clang against a reeling cuspidor. His mouth full of sawdust he glared over his shoulder — But only for an instant, for Abe was upon him. By main strength he yanked him up and then slammed his open palm across Dyson's bearded face — back and forth with stinging impact until sheer pain and fury made him crash out his right fist.

Abe countered it instantly and whipped a savage punch straight into Dyson's middle. He doubled up with an explosion of breath, to straighten again from an uppercut to the chin. Dazed, he fell to his knees, gasping for breath.

'Mebby before I've finished with you I'll knock some confession out of you,' Abe panted. 'That's what I'm striving for — right here where there are plenty of witnesses!'

'Confession?' Dyson snarled, slowly straightening up and holding his middle. 'Even if there wus anythin' to confess to, which there ain't, you haven't got the power to do anythin' about it! Why don't yuh get outa here while yore in one piece, Feather-Fist?'

'It'd make more sense if I said that of *you*,' Abe retorted. 'I think I've proved by now that I'm no feather-fist — an' as fur my having no power to make use of any confession you give, take a look at this.'

Abe held out his palm, the marshal's badge in the centre of it. Dyson stared incredulously at it, then up at Abe's grim face.

'So yore a marshal, huh? One of the bright boys set to chase us? An' that yeller streak was nothin' more than an act — '

'Sent to chase you?' Abe cut in quickly. 'Why? What need would I have to chase you if you haven't done anythin' wrong? I reckon yore accusin yourself out of your own mouth, Dyson, an' I'll — '

Abe broke off as the back-bar mirror splintered under the impact of a bullet. He beheld Lynch Corbett with a smoking gun in his hand.

'There's a durned sight too much talkin' goin' on around here and too little action,' Lynch said. He looked at Dyson. 'Yore supposed to be sheriff, but I'm yore deputy. If yuh can't handle a situation like this mebby I'd better do it meself.'

Dyson stared, plainly caught on the

hop. Abe, too, was doing a bit of swift thinking. He even found himself wondering if this was not perhaps the moment Lynch had selected to break with his partner. That the two had no love for each other he had known for some time.

'I never got into a situation I couldn't handle,' Dyson spat at him. 'I'm just taken by surprise that this guy's a marshal — '

'Aw, put your damned cards on the table!' Lynch said sourly, still holding his gun. 'He knows who we are and there ain't no point in trying to avoid it any longer. We've two lines of action we can take. Rub this marshal out and keep our hold on this by sheer force — an' there's plenty here right now who'll fight along with us; or else we can throw everythin' up and do just as the marshal tells us.'

'Have you gone loco, Lynch?' Alroyd demanded, using the gunman's right name for the first time. 'You can never hold a whole town down by force, no matter how many you get. 'Sides, wipin' out a marshal is dangerous meat. You'll have a whole army of 'em down here after you. Mountain's End'll become nothin' but a battleground.'

Lynch shrugged. 'Mebby. So what? We're both wanted anyways, so the fight we put up doesn't matter. Down here we're mighty comfortable — or were 'til this critter moved in. I don't see us givin' it up that easily.'

Dyson hesitated, plainly trying to make up his mind. Then before he could do so Lynch's gun exploded again. This time the bullet hit the watching barkeep and dropped him at the back of the counter.

Abe wheeled — then as he caught sight of Alroyd full of a questioning stare he gave him a quick nod. Immediately Alroyd whipped out his own guns.

'Fur as I'm concerned this has gone far enough!' he shouted. 'I'm with law and order an' always have bin. Get these hoodlums outa here before we're so hamstrung we can't move!'

And that set fire to the dynamite with a vengeance. Alroyd's supporters immediately moved into the positions he had already assigned to them. They tipped up the tables and used them as screens, firing over the tops of them at the men who had elected to come under Dyson's banner. In many ways they had the advantage since they scuttled behind the heavy barrier of the bar counter and sniped round the side or over the top of it.

'I reckon it's the only way to decide the issue,' Alroyd muttered, as Abe came beside him, his remaining gun in his hand. 'Even if you hadn't turned up an' worked out a plan it would ha' bin the only way to force a show-down and get law an order back agen — '

A bullet splintered the top of the table-edge close to his ear. He ducked quickly.

'Do what you like with the rest of these hoodlums,' Abe muttered, 'but try and avoid hitting Lynch and Dyson — particularly Dyson. I want him specially.'

'Okay . . . ' Alroyd peeped swiftly round the table-edge and fired. An unwary supporter of Dyson got the bullet in his forehead and collapsed behind the counter.

Abe himself did not make much effort to join in the fight. He kept constantly on the alert for signs of Lynch or Dyson making a getaway, but at the moment the two gunmen were too intent on trying to cling onto their brief authority to think of making a dash. At least Dyson was. Lynch had his own ideas.

'I reckon this is nothin' but plumb crazy,' he snapped to Dyson, as he paused to quickly reload his guns. 'This shootin' match can go on for ever, and even if we happen to win it what do we get?'

'Everythin'!' Dyson clicked the chambers over quickly. 'I guess that's your main trouble, Lynch; yuh've got no imagination. Once we've won this battle — and we're goin' ter! — there won't be anybody in Mountain's End who'll dare to

194

challenge us. This show-down is a-goin' to establish us fur good.'

'Mebby . . . ' Lynch dodged down and then fired relentlessly from cover. 'Yuh seem to have forgotten about the marshal.'

Dyson grinned. 'There won't be no marshal by the time this is over. He'll go with the rest of these bright boys who think we're not fit t'run the place.'

'And when his boys come to investigate — ?' Lynch sighted carefully and dropped one of Alroyd's men.

'We'll hold out against them, too. We got guns, ain't we?'

'Can't go on for ever,' Lynch growled, reloading. 'I'm all fur gettin' out, cleanin' up that mausoleum bonanza, and then hittin' the trail.'

Dyson eyed him coldly. 'Listen, Lynch, yuh've done nothin' but belly-ache ever since we took over here, an' I'm more'n sick uv it! We're stayin' right here if it's at all possible, an that's an order.'

'Yeah?' Lynch's eyes narrowed. 'Since

when did you start givin' *me* orders? I please meself what I do, an if I decide to break fur it and head outa town I'll do it. I sure won't stop an' ask you.'

Dyson glanced about him. His men were too preoccupied with firing and dodging to pay any attention to the argument so close to them.

'I reckon,' Dyson said, 'that that's what yuh've had on your mind fur long enough. Ditchin' me and gettin' to that bonanza as quick as yuh can. I'm takin' care uv that right now.'

Instinctively Lynch jerked his gun round, prepared for trouble — but his movement was not swift enough. Dyson fired deliberately, knowing perfectly well that his own particular shots would never be noticed in the general staccato. Nobody even glanced as Lynch clapped his hands to his chest and fell heavily half under the counter.

'Guess we're a good man short,' Dyson muttered, edging to the gun-hawk nearest him. 'They got my pardner. How long can we hold out?'

'Not long.' The other man gave him a grim glance. 'There's a limit to the ammunition, sheriff, and if those men shootin' for Alroyd and the marshal have got more slugs than us we'll be on the receiving end of a rope before we know it.'

Dyson tightened his lips, doing his best to make up his mind. Moving along, he peered round the side of the bar counter and weighed up the situation. By this time the saloon was more or less in ruins. The only fixtures left free of gun-blast were the lamps, since both sides needed light to see what they were doing. In other directions tables were split and scarred, bottles and glasses were shattered into fragments, the mirrors were huge daggers of glass hanging out of their frames, while upon the floor sawdust was drifting in the pools of spirit and beer which had collected.

'They show no sign of let-up, sheriff!'

Dyson turned his head as the man he had just spoken to crept to his side.

'Mebby they figgered on somethin' like this and laid in extra bullets,' the man added worriedly. 'I don't like it. We can't go much beyond five minutes more.'

'Keep on firin',' Dyson said. 'I've got an idea which might swing the balance. Keep me covered whilst I creep round to the back. I'm a-goin' to set fire to the joint on the enemy's side. That'll bring 'em into the open and mebby we can just finish 'em.'

'Okay — ' The man hesitated. 'But look, if yuh burn the place down, what happens? We're fightin' to keep you as sheriff and preserve this property yuh've bought. If yuh burn it down — '

'We build it again,' Dyson said. 'We'll pretty nearly have to anyways, considerin' the mess it's in — Just do as I've told yuh.'

The man shrugged and returned to his former vantage point — so Dyson began moving. He scrambled round the back of the bar counter and then watched his chance. The moment there was a lull in the smoke-choked expanse he darted from cover and dropped behind a nearby uptilted table. In this position he was at the top end of the 'no-man's land' and within reach of one of the kerosene wall lamps.

But fast though he had moved he had not done it unobserved. Abe, doing nothing else but keep on the look-out, had seen his action. He inclined his head to nearby Alroyd.

'Dyson's up to something,' he murmured. 'An' I don't see any sign of Lynch either . . . '

Alroyd glanced quickly towards the spot Abe indicated, visible through a gun-hole in the table top they were using as a shield — then abruptly Dyson took the risk of jumping up, grabbing the oil lamp, and hurling it. Instantly Alroyd's gun flashed up but Abe grabbed his arm.

'Hold it! I still want him — '

'But he's setting the darned place on fire — '

'I know. Deal with it as you can. I'm

keeping an eye on Dyson. Not bad strategy on his part — escape in the confusion.'

Abe had guessed correctly. Flames had already spurted from the fallen lamp and were driving Alroyd's men out of cover, and into the whining shower of bullets from Dyson's side. But Dyson himself, struggling through the smoke and fallen furniture with the flames forming a good screen, was making his way to the batwings. Abe watched him intently — then the instant the gunhawk had got beyond the doors he got up as far as his knees.

'Deal with this how you can,' he said briefly to Alroyd. 'Get those hoodlums down and out if possible. I'll be back later. I'm after Dyson — '

Abe wasted no more time. Ducking and wriggling he too reached the batwings and so out onto the board-walk. He was just in time to catch a glimpse of Dyson riding hell-for-leather down the lamp-lighted street — then distance began to swallow him as he hit the northward trail out of town.

By this time the fire within the saloon was the real thing. Abe looked at it grimly. The flames had seized the sun-rotten timbers and were devouring the roof. A window went in pieces as fire hit it. Within, there was a mad pandemonium of shouts and revolver shots. Down the street men and women were appearing, drawn by the noise and belching smoke.

Abe waited no longer. He hurried down the steps and swung to the saddle of his horse. Quickly untying the reins he jerked the animal's head round and then began to head out of town as fast as he could go. He had to leave the fire and fighting behind him, but he was reasonably sure that a stalwart like Alroyd, and the tough men he had chosen to help him, would finally get the better of the situation . . .

7

Presently galloping out onto the main northward trail, Abe drew rein and looked sharply about him in the rising moonlight. As far as his eyes were concerned he could not detect anybody, but to his ears on the still night there floated the slowly diminishing sound of horse's hoofs. Dyson was evidently moving fast, and still travelling north which could only mean the mausoleum was his destination.

Abe grinned to himself and started his horse forward again. He kept a constant watch ahead, but in the uncertain light failed to detect any sign of his quarry — but the constant pauses he made did bring him that unmistakable beat of a galloping horse moving ever onwards.

Satisfied by now that the mausoleum was indeed Dyson's destination Abe broke away from the main trail and instead travelled cross-country until he was within half-a-mile of the Redskin ruins. Here he dropped from his horse, tied the reins to a tree stump, and then continued silently on foot through the moonlight. A matter of ten minutes brought him to the outskirts of the ruins and here he slid down behind one of the rocks and surveyed carefully. There was no sign of anybody, or even a horse. Evidently his cross-country detour had put him ahead of Dyson, unless perhaps the outlaw had not been heading for this spot after all. This possibility brought a frown to Abe's face — then he realised it was hardly tenable. The mausoleum *must* be Dyson's destination. There were no towns that he could reach, no ranches that would give him sanctuary — not in this northward direction . . .

Then gradually, and faintly, there came on the air that familiar drumming of hoofs. Abe crouched down and waited, to be finally rewarded by the sight of Dyson astride his horse, which had now dropped to a canter, approaching from the desert trail. At the outermost rim of stones he alighted, tied the reins to a boulder, and then cautiously advanced. The faint moonbeams reflected from his gun barrel.

Not a sound; not a whisper. Dyson could be forgiven for thinking that he was utterly alone. He moved now with an added touch of boldness, tripping occasionally over loose stones, and he kept on going until he reached the worn steps leading down into the main vault. The moment he had descended from sight Abe rose, pulled out his gun, and glided after him. He did not, however, descend into the vault. Instead he paused at one of the many holes, which pierced the vault roof, and peered through. There was the dim flicker of a tinder-flame below, constantly renewed as Dyson kept on the prowl, picking up bits of gold from the floor.

For a time Abe watched, then he quietly made his way to the vault steps and crept down into the darkness.

When he finally got to the entrance of the vault Dyson's back was to him, a tinder flickering over his head, as he searched the walls carefully, presumably for more traces of gold.

Abe surveyed the badly lighted vault quickly. According to his plan, and the arrangements he had made with Captain Derriker, there ought to be two or three rangers concealed down here to overhear the confession Abe intended forcing out of Dyson. But the more he looked, the more worried Abe became. Though there were many vantage points where men could have hidden there was not a sign of one anywhere.

What then, had gone wrong? Derriker surely had not failed him? Unless, perhaps, they had found some new neighbouring hiding place just as useful and still within earshot. Abe just did not know what to think. The only thing for it seemed to be to go ahead as he had promised to do and trust to luck that the witnesses would reveal themselves when necessary.

Silently, Abe moved forward, gun ready.

'If yore lookin' for gold, Dyson, I shouldn't waste any more time.'

Dyson swung round, his hand flying to his gun, until he realised he was covered.

'You, huh?' He came forward, still holding the tinder; then he abruptly threw it down and plunged the place into darkness.

Abe thanked his stars that he had already anticipated this move. He had taken note of a nearby tall stone, and the instant the light vanished he darted to cover. Not a second too soon for Dyson's gun flashed and blazed at the spot where Abe had been standing. Abe remained motionless, not giving his position away either by breathing or firing. In any case he had no wish to put a bullet through Dyson — not just yet.

'So yore still yeller, huh?' came Dyson's jeering voice out of the darkness. 'I might have known it, Feather-Fist. You know where I am by my voice,

206

an' yore too scared to do anythin' about it! Okay, then I'll start to find you — an' I won't miss, neither.'

There was a sound of movement. Abe waited, ready to play the blind man's bluff game as far as possible. He started to move in and around the sacrificial stones, occasionally making a noise which compelled Dyson to change direction and start heading towards him. All the time Abe kept his attention on the oblong of grey which denoted the entrance door of the vault. He was prepared to fly into instant action if for a moment he saw Dyson's silhouette dashing outside.

But Dyson did not attempt anything like that. Since he had not been shot at he was reasonably sure that Abe had reverted to his earlier timidity — and what was more important to Dyson, he meant finishing this meddlesome marshal once and for all. After a while he fired a couple of experimental shots at where he thought Abe was concealed. He was wrong by several yards.

Abe grinned to himself at the wide miss. At least it had shown him where Dyson was, so he prepared himself to spring and grapple, bring this cat and mouse business to an end. Darkness did not matter. He did not need light to hammer the senses out of the gunman, nor to extract a confession from him. The only irritating worry, to Abe, was where the witnesses *were*. He was prepared to swear by now that they just couldn't be in the vault —

Such were the split-second thoughts that passed through his mind as he prepared himself to leap. Only to his amazement his leap never started. The step backwards he took in the dark to catapult himself forward had the effect of plunging him into a bottomless blackness.

He seemed to sail down for an interminable distance, finally crashing onto solid rock. It nearly knocked the senses out of him and he gasped at the anguish of jarred bones and bruised flesh. Where he was he had not the faintest idea, but he was aware of a peculiar sulphuric odour around his nostrils. The more he inhaled it the more he felt his senses swimming — a dizziness out of all proportion to the fall he had taken. He stirred weakly in the blackness, even tried to shout to Dyson for help — though he instinctively knew he would not get it — then in the midst of his efforts he passed out altogether . . .

The next thing he knew — how long afterwards he had no idea — a wet cloth was passing over his forehead and there was a different kind of smell. Garlic! He opened his eyes and looked around him upon some kind of vault, illuminated by a guttering, kerosene-soaked cloth.

'What in tarnation goes on?' Abe whispered, struggling to his elbow, and then he became aware of the source of the garlic odour. Right beside him was the grizzled, know-all face of old Drygulch.

'Lucky fur you I follow a critter

around when I don't like him,' Drygulch commented, spitting sideways. 'Like as not yuh'd have passed out fur good otherwise. Same as these other guys down here.'

Still unable to decide whether he was in the midst of a dream or not Abe looked around him. His attention was immediately diverted to three men lying nearby, their shirts and badges immediately proclaiming them as marshals.

'They're — they're not — ?' Abe looked startled.

'Dead?' Drygulch nodded solemnly. 'Yes, *sir!*'

'But how did it *happen*? What's going on?'

'Fur as I can make out — gas. Volcanic gas. I've come across it many a time in me wanderings. Fatal if yuh breathe it in fur too long. I smelled it the minnit I got down here, but I managed to divert it.'

Abe moved uncomfortably, aware now of the numberless bruises he had received in his fall — but as far as he could tell there were no bones broken.

'Divert it?' he repeated at length. 'How'd you manage that?'

'It wus comin' through one of the blow-holes there.' Drygulch nodded towards the back of the cave. 'I jammed in a stone and me neckcloth. That stopped it. I reckon it'll find some other way out. As for these guys — ' He looked towards the men lying nearby. 'I guess they couldn't ha' bin wise to what was happenin'. They must ha' come here and the gas put 'em out before they discovered where it came frum. Not like me: I'm usta things like that an' I know where to look. I reckon mebby I can hold me breath, too, as long as any man livin'.'

With the old prospector's help Abe made a sudden effort and gradually struggled to his feet.

'I suppose the gas wasn't strong enough to float into the upper cave,' he said, thinking. 'That would be why neither Dyson nor me noticed it.'

'Dyson? Oh, the bearded sheriff!

Yeah, that would be the reason. There's a lot of vent holes in the ceilin' of this cave which would carry the gas off afore it reached the upper parts. Like I sed, it was lucky fur you I kept me eye on that sheriff. I'd figgered on givin' him a beatin' up, same as he gave me, so I stuck around Mountain's End when I was supposed to have headed fur any place else. I saw you come, an' I saw him. When there was only him came outa the vault I had to do a bit of quick thinkin'. Looked ter me as though he'd finished yuh. I let him go and came to look. That was when I found the gas — an' these other fellers lyin' around.'

Abe swore. 'Then the whole damned plan's fallen to bits since Dyson's got away. I can pretty well see now what happened. These men either found — or made — a hole in the vault floor and came down here to listen to the confession I was going to try and get from Dyson. Instead of that they were knocked out by gas. I can't understand why they didn't discover it.'

'Probably 'cos they wus absorbed in somethin' else,' Drygulch said enigmatically. 'An' that hole in the floor is a natural collapse, frum what I've seen. Mebby these three stood together on that area an' the lot broke through.'

'Uh-huh, could be. I wondered where the hell I was going to — ' Abe's expression changed. 'How'd you mean? Those three were absorbed in somethin' else? Their job was to be around when and if a confession could be forced out of Dyson. They just *couldn't* have anythin' else to occupy 'em.'

'There ain't no sane man livin' who'll turn his back on gold,' Drygulch said. 'And I reckon you musta bin holdin' out on me when you sed this weren't no bonanza. Take a look fur yuhself!'

For the first time Abe took a definite interest in his surroundings. He followed the sweep of old Drygulch's arm and in the flickering light he became aware that there were gleaming veins running through the rocky walls. Also upon the floor were small chips of yellow metal. Hardly daring to believe what he saw, Abe picked up one of the lumps and weighed it in his palm.

'Suffering cats! Gold!' He swung, astounded.

'Yeah, more gold than I ever did see! I guess that was what them rangers saw and they were so busy looking around they didn't notice the gas 'til it was too late. Mebby they even didn't let it escape 'til they accidentally pulled away some rock from a bung-hole. That don't matter now: what *does* matter is that we've happened on one hell of a bonanza. It musta bin buried fur ages under the mausoleum.'

'And, come to think of it,' Abe said slowly, 'that stream where I used to wash dirt could very easily pass underground here. This might be where the gold was washed from.'

'Stream?' Drygulch repeated; then Abe glanced at him.

'Never mind: just thinkin' out loud —'

'This is one bonanza I'm *not* goin' to be talked out of,' Drygulch commented pointedly. 'I kept quiet as you sed 'cos I thought you meant it when yuh sed there wasn't a real bonanza here. Now I've seen this I'm hornin' in on it.'

'An' yore welcome,' Abe grinned. 'Old-timer, there's more than enough here for the both of us for life. An' I still ask that you don't tell a soul. This is yours an' mine.'

'Check,' Drygulch grinned.

'But this isn't the end of the road,' Abe continued, his face suddenly grim. 'I've a job to finish. I've Dyson to nail, and now he's gone from here I don't know where to look for him. I'm sort of wonderin' why he went as he did — '

'Probably he investigated the hole yuh fell through and got a whiff of that gas. As fur where he's gone, that ain't much of a problem.'

'Glad you think so. The desert's always seemed to me to be a pretty big place.'

'Not so big that yuh can't read it when yuh've had as much experience as I have. I'm a sight older than you, son, and a lot more skilful. We'll find that critter all right We *both* want him, remember, and that makes a difference.'

'The Tucson authorities will have to be told about these men,' Abe added, glancing towards them.

'They will be — but I don't see that it's urgent. They'll never be any deader than they are now. Right now we'd better get outa here and close up the hole in the floor as best we can — No!' Drygulch snapped his fingers suddenly. 'Fust we want these three men taken inter the vault above and left there, *then* we cover the hole in. Otherwise, when more Tucson men arrive to see what happened they'll see that gold vault as well an' I ain't in the mood for us to share out. We can say that gas escaped into the vault an' keep quiet about this one. Yes, sir!'

Abe nodded. 'Let's get busy. I'll go up first and drop down a rope.'

Altogether it took the pair of them an hour to get the three bodies into the upper vault and then cover up the hole. Their gruesome task finished they climbed the steps and emerged under the night sky.

'Now what do we do?' Abe asked, quite content to leave the issue to the knowledgeable old-timer.

'Nothin',' Drygulch responded calmly. 'We're not goin' to git anywhere ridin' around by night, an it ain't possible to follow a trail until daylight. Fur another thing we need some sleep — 'specially you, after that tumble you took.'

'But while we're wasting time sleeping, Drygulch, Dyson can cover the hell of a distance.'

Not without ample food and water. He's only got what was in his saddle-bag, and his horse needs rest. He'll stop somewheres in the night and be movin' agen at sun-up. That's when we move too. You take the first doss; I'll stay on look-out in case anythin' happens.'

Abe said no more. Drygulch's mature outlook on the situation was the only one which could be accepted. He and

Abe both collected their bedrolls from their horses, and whilst Abe found himself drifting into sleep the old-timer remained alert, smoking a particularly foul pipe and listening to the faint sounds of the sand lizards and the distant scream of a mountain lion.

Some hours before dawn Abe awoke and took over his own spell of duty. Nothing disturbed the calmness of the night and, at last, the daylight began to appear and with it the thick cotton-wool dawn mist that enveloped these regions like a blanket . . . As though he had been bestirred by an alarm clock Drygulch awoke and, following a brief wash from the hoarded contents of his water barrel, he set about the job of digging out chow for breakfast. Abe did exactly the same thing and, as the mists were dispersing before the first golden shafts of the sun, they ate their respective meals.

'How you figger getting on Dyson's track, I don't know,' Abe admitted, staring out towards the desert. 'I never knew sand to leave a trail worth following. It changes hourly with the wind drift.'

'You sure are plumb certain that critter's taken to the desert, ain't you?' Drygulch asked. 'Start askin' yuhself: if you wus in *his* place, with limited supplies, would you take to the desert?'

'Not from choice, no — simply because it's the safest place when you're on the run.'

'There's the helluv a lot of safer places, son. In the desert yuh've got no shade frum the sun, no cover frum anybody lookin' fur you — and above all the water problem. Y'can wipe out all three problems by takin' to the mountains, an' I'll stake all I've got — bonanza included — that that's just what that no-account sheriff would do.'

'The range around Mountain's End, you mean?'

'Sure. That's the best place. Not only can he keep hid, but he can have a good idea what's goin' on as well. I figger I'm right, judgin' it frum what I'd do meself. The desert's dangerous, an' he daren't show up in any town, so the mountains look like a good bet. Sooner we find out the sooner we know.'

Abe glanced towards the not far distant range and then frowned.

'There's another angle to that, Drygulch,' he said, getting to his feet. 'From the mountains Dyson can command a view of anybody approaching. If he sees us, we're dead pigeons.'

'We gotta risk that. The main foothills is some two miles from the mountains themselves. The desert track ends at the foothills. If we follow the trail that far and find any sign of a horse having bin there recent — and the hoof-marks'll show up in the soil and sand of the foothills — we can think further. Dyson can't fire a gun over two miles range, so we'll be safe enough.'

Abe did not comment further. As seemed natural to him, Drygulch had worked out everything to the last detail. In a few more minutes the pair had packed everything up and were on their way. To commence with the going was easy since the sun had not fully risen over the still dispersing mists.

As Abe had expected there was no sign of a trail leading from the mausoleum — at least not on the desert side. On the opposite side lay the pasture lands, but a brief examination here revealed no sign of a horse's prints.

'Yeah,' Drygulch mused, as they rode steadily on, 'I'm more'n sure he'd take to the mountains.'

'Can but hope,' Abe murmured. Then after a moment: 'See anything of that fire at the Naughty Lady last night?'

'Sure did. They was just a-startin' it as I left town t'follow the sheriff. I kept ways off the trail an' saw you pursuin' him. But you didn't see me, huh?' And the old-timer chuckled to himself.

'I'm just wondering,' Abe said slowly. 'Whether the town will still be standing or if the fire mightn't have burned it to ashes. If there's nothing but ruin quite a few people besides us will be headin' towards the mountains.'

Drygulch shook his head. 'Take more'n a saloon fire to set a town alight. The town'll still be there even though the saloon mightn't be.'

About an hour later they had come within seeing distance of the town and confirmation of the old prospector's words. The main buildings and stores were still standing but the saloon and neighbouring ramshackles had been burned to the ground.

'Well, the sheriff sure lost the lot,' Drygulch commented, preparing to move on again. 'I reckon he made that saloon his headquarters an' his main source of income. Without it he may just as well be on his way.'

'Wonder who won the fight?' Abe reflected, toying with the idea of a quick visit to Alroyd — then remembering the importance of his own mission, and the fact that the previous night's battle might *not* have gone in favour of Alroyd, he changed his mind. In silence he continued to ride swiftly beside Drygulch until they eventually reached the trail's end which led only one way — straight to the mountains.

'Right now,' Drygulch said, his eyes screwed up as he surveyed the looming height, 'we're probably under observation — but that's one of the risks. We've gotta find if there's a trail of a horse anywheres around here.'

So both he and Abe dropped from their mounts and began to search carefully. Abe for his part failed to discover anything, but this was probably because he did not use the immensely thorough tactics of the old prospector. For Drygulch was not content with just looking. He turned stones and studied them, traced over the hard ground with his fingers, and even studied the stunted bushes for signs of odd horse hairs where an animal could have brushed by. And it was because of such tactics that he presently came to a spot where a hoof-mark was visible. Only one, where the earth was softer than usual, and this one pointed in the direction of the mountains.

'The cayuse owning that shoe was doing a good gallop,' Drygulch commented, straightening up from his examination. 'The front of the shoe is deeper impressed than the back, an' towards those mountains we'll soon come within range of a gun.'

'But where does it get us?' Abe questioned, staring at the range. 'Those mountains cover the whale of a lot of space and distance. And there's another thing — once we advance that's a sure sign.'

'Yeah — but not if we go round the back way,' Drygulch grinned. 'It's worth a gamble to see if we *can* spot the sheriff.'

Abe looked dubious as they returned to their horses. 'Did it ever occur to you, Drygulch, that it might take weeks to do that?'

'Lissen, son, there's still a lot yuh've got to learn — 'specially since you've become a marshal — '

'Only pro tem. I've had no trainin'.'

'More than obvious, meanin' no disrespect. I'm just sayin' that I ain't come on this chase fur the fun of it, but because I think we can find the man we're lookin' fur. He's bound to give himself away finally — 'specially by night.'

'Why by night?'

'Two reasons. One, it's hell-fired cold by night and no man can survive in the mountains without warmth. That demands a fire.'

'I agree — but probably inside a cave with a bed-blanket over the opening to hide the glow.'

'Hide the glow mebby, but the *smoke's* gotta go someplace or else choke our ornery sheriff to death. If we don't see the smoke in the moonlight — an' there's plenty uv chance tha we might — we can probably smell it. Leastways I can — an' once I do I'll just follow my nose. We'll find him, one way or the other. I'll stake everythin' on it.'

Still with many doubts in his mind

Abe clambered back onto his horse and thereafter he kept behind the old prospector as he rode steadily away from the mountains — a good two miles beyond their furthest limit in fact — and then began to double back in a wide semicircle. By noon half the distance to the rear of the range had been covered and a halt was made for lunch.

'I'm wondering,' Abe said, as he and Drygulch sat chewing their tinned provisions, 'If it wouldn't be a good idea for one of us — or at any rate me — to go back to Tucson and get a couple of men along. If we get Dyson I want some witnesses in authority present to hear that confession I mean gettin' out of him.'

The prospector chewed for a while and then nodded. 'Mebby it wouldn't be a bad idea at that, while yore doin' it I'll get busy trying to locate the sheriff. Once I've done it I'll return to this spot and wait — then I can lead the bunch of yer.'

So it was decided. Immediately the meal was over Abe set off on his long journey, rapidly leaving the mountain region behind in the glare of the afternoon sun, but not before he had taken full note of the exact position to which he was to return — and whilst he continued on his lonely journey Drygulch rode solemnly on, either dragging at his foul pipe or lambently chewing a quid of garlic. He was alert for the least sign of danger — but none came.

So he completed the circuit of the mountain range's end and began to ride to the rear of it, always moving upwards, along steep rimrocks and acclivities, until by the early evening he had reached a summit point some thousand or more feet below the highest pinnacle but at an altitude good enough to give him a grand view of the rugged slopes on both sides of him.

'Yeah,' he murmured to his pinto, leaning on the saddle-horn and surveying. 'I reckon this is just the spot fur a watch-tower.'

Satisfied with his vantage point he descended from his horse and made his preparations for a makeshift camp. By the time he had finished it was sun-down. His back against a spur he ate a meal, drank the remains of some cold coffee so as not to give away his position by smoke or flame, and then he dispassionately sucked at his pipe and waited — watching, watching, always watching.

He saw the lights of Mountain's End begin to appear, until the whole ramshackle township was clearly picked out, except for the gaping blot where the saloon had been. But the mountains themselves remained dark, the upper and lower heights wreathed in gathering mist and the centre line clear. On the chill wind which came sweeping down was borne the refreshing aroma of juniper and pine.

Drygulch still sat on, drawing one of his bedroll blankets about him, his wrinkled, tireless eyes constantly on the move. He was fully prepared for the vigil he had undertaken and if there *was* anything to be seen he was quite convinced he would not miss it when it came. The only thing that worried him was the necessity of sleep. That would come later. At the moment the wiry old man of desert and plain was wide awake.

A light! The merest pinpoint glimmer and almost instantly extinguished, but in the soft darkness of the mountains it glinted for a few brief seconds with diamond brightness. Drygulch's eyes switched to it even as it expired. He kept his gaze fixed on that position for a moment or two, then looked above the spot to the mist-wreathed pinnacle which stood like a bleak signpost to the light's position.

'Reckon you an' me got some travelling to do,' Drygulch remarked to the pinto, as he got to his feet. 'That wus either some mug lighting a cigarette an' fergettin' for the moment ter keep his hand round the flame, else he's thinkin' of lightin' a fire. Can't think he'd be crazy enough ter do that.'

In this Drygulch guessed correctly for no sign of fire followed. He did not wait any longer. Keeping the pinnacle as his goal he urged his sure-footed little horse forward, slowly and cautiously. He was not at all sure but that he would not come suddenly upon the position of the light. In the blackness he had not been able to assess the distance . . .

So he progressed, until the rimrock path he was following suddenly opened out on a flat, tableland area with the upwardly flung mountains towering up behind.

'This might be it,' he muttered to the horse, and drew rein. 'Stay right here until I come back.'

Ears flicked and the faithful pinto remained as though carved in stone. Without a sound Drygulch crept forward, and the further he progressed the more obvious it became that this flat area was actually a titanic thin-edged rock jutting out into space. At its furthest extremity was a sheer drop of probably a thousand feet to the lower foothills; whilst behind lay the backdrop of the mountains themselves. In the face of the mountain were the dark eyes of caves and it was presumably from one of these that that transient glint of light had come.

Drygulch was not fool enough to go too close to the caves in case he gave himself away. Instead he took up a position behind a rock some hundred feet distant and watched intently. His eyes, thoroughly accustomed by now to the darkness, presently descried that the central cave opening was darker than the others, which probably meant that a blanket had been drawn across it. Satisfied on this point he risked going closer — and still closer, until he was directly outside the cave itself. Pressed flat against the mountain wall he listened intently.

For a long time he heard nothing, then quite suddenly there were the sounds of movement. There was no time to dodge back; no time to do anything. Drygulch froze against the wall and held his breath.

It was unmistakably Dyson who emerged. The darkness of his beard was distinguishable against the white of his face. He came out cautiously, using the blanket to smother the dim fan of light from an oil lamp he was evidently carrying in his equipment . . . All he did when he actually came outside was throw a couple of empty meat tins — or so they seemed to be — over the edge of the distant rock lip and then shake the coffee grounds from a metal pot. He never even saw Drygulch, mainly because the light of the lamp in the cave had made Dyson comparatively blind in the intense dark of these mountain heights.

With the same stealth he returned inside the cave and the blanket closed tightly. Drygulch relaxed and drew his sleeve over his face — then he silently made his way back to his horse.

'The guy we want is right there,

feller,' he told the animal. 'I guess he'll stay there fur awhile until he thinks the coast is clear enough to begin movin' on — which won't be fur a day or two mebby. Meantime we've gotta go back to where we started frum so's we can be ready fur the marshal . . . On your way, pal.'

★ ★ ★

Abe Jones did not ride back from Tucson that same night. There were limits to his physical endurance. Once he arrived in the town he bedded down in a rooming-house for the night, then in the morning went to Derriker's headquarters and explained the situation. In consequence three further men were quickly detailed and Abe rode back with them through most of the morning and part of the afternoon, arriving at the spot where Drygulch was waiting when the sun was just commencing to wester.

'Any luck?' Abe asked eagerly, dropping from the saddle.

'Sure thing. No tellin' how long it will hold out, but if we act tonight we oughta be in time.' Drygulch jerked his head to a distant pinnacle. 'That's the marker. Right below that the so-called sheriff's hidin' in a cave . . . ' and he gave the details of his night's activities.

'One hunch that came off!' Abe exclaimed in delight. 'We'd better start that way right now.'

'An' make it straight an' plain that yore coming?' Drygulch demanded. 'That ain't sensible. Wait till it's dark and then follow me. I know the way — an' you can trust me.'

'He's right there, Abe,' one of the rangers said, nodding. 'Meantime we'd better ride over to that mausoleum and bury those three boys of ours. We'll have to check up, of course.'

'Okay.' Abe was obviously reluctant. 'You stay here, Drygulch, and keep your eyes open in case Dyson makes a break for it.'

'Ain't no reason why he should, fur as I can see. He knows the townsfolk an' rangers must be rattin' for him by now. He'll sit pretty until chow runs out — depends how much he had in his saddlebag. I'll stop, though, just in case.'

Abe nodded and swung back to the saddle. His three compatriots did likewise and the ride to the mausoleum began. As Abe had hoped the three men took his word for it that the previous trio had been overwhelmed by gas in the upper vault, and made no attempt to look further. The burials were completed by sun-down, then after a rest and food the return trip to Drygulch's 'base' was made. The old-timer was still there, chewing garlic and watching the roseate flame of the sunset against the mountains.

'Nothin' stirrin',' he announced. 'Soon as the night drops we begin movin'.'

'Any particular ideas as to how we tackle Dyson?' one of the men questioned.

'Simply surround his cave and order him to come out or be shot,' one of the other men said briefly. 'All you c'n do.'

'That way you'll arrest him all right,' Abe agreed, 'but it isn't good enough for me. I'm out to get a confession from him, even if I haveta beat his brains out to do it.'

'That isn't the law,' the third man said grimly. 'Rough stuff is out. A straight arrest is our job.'

'Yuh might let *me* speak too,' Drygulch put in. 'I don't give a blue cent for the law, an' yuh can lock me up afterwards if it gives yuh any satisfaction — but I want yuh to leave me be and stick around while I go to work. I'll make that mug talk, but good — and I'll take plenty of repayment fur that beatin' up he gave me too. I got it all worked out. A man c'n do a lot of thinkin' when he sits alone — like I do more often than not.'

'But give us *some* idea,' one of the rangers pleaded. 'We've got the law to uphold and — '

'Aw, to heck with the law! Leave me be, can't yuh?'

To argue with a wizened old relic like Drygulch was useless, as Abe and the rangers soon found out — so finally they gave way to him and, when darkness had completely fallen, they mounted their horses and followed his lead over the rough slopes and acclivities until eventually they arrived at the edge of the tableland.

'Right, this is it,' Drygulch said, slipping from the saddle. 'He's in that central cave there. Keep me covered and watch what I'm going to do. You'll get your chance, son,' he added over his shoulder to Abe.

Abe muttered something but did as he was told. With the three rangers beside him he watched intently as Drygulch crossed the flat rockery. At the centre of the big area he unloosed a lariat from around his shoulders, noosed it, then held it ready for action in his right hand. In his left he held his gun.

He fired once, straight into the air, a deafening, reverberating explosion in

237

the enclosed space. Almost instantly Dyson came hurtling out of his hiding place, gun ready and head darting for evidence of the disturbance. Slickly the noose descended over his shoulders and drew taut, nailing his arms to his sides. He fired once wildly — and missed.

'Howdy, sheriff,' Drygulch greeted cynically, and in one move whipped the gun from Dyson's hand. 'Kind uv bin wantin' to meet up with you agen.'

'So it's you!' Dyson roared. 'Why you dirty saddle tramp, I'll durned soon — '

'No you won't.' And despite his age Drygulch landed a pretty vicious left hook that overbalanced Dyson completely. Before he could get up again, due to the imprisoning rope round his arm, he found his ankles lashed together as Drygulch drew the rope down sharply and knotted it.

'So fur so good,' Drygulch grinned: 'I reckon this is where yuh start learnin' a thing or two.'

Puzzled, Abe and the rangers continued to watch. Dyson, trussed very effectually, also gazed in silence as Drygylch took the loose end of the rope and fastened it round a rock spur; then by main strength he grabbed Dyson's shoulders and hauled him towards the edge of the rock-slab.

'Hey, yuh dirty skunk!' Dyson screamed. 'What's the idea?'

'Yuh'll see in a moment, git over — !'

A final shove and Dyson rolled over the edge of the slab and dropped into the void. The rope brought him up with a painful jerk. Swinging face down in the abyss, suspended horizontally by the rope holding arms and ankles, he had either to stare into that awful gulf below or shut his eyes. Meantime he spun in a slow circle and the dizzying effect was terrifying in the extreme.

'I reckon that's where yuh should have bin long ago,' Drygulch yelled at him; then he glanced as Abe and the rangers gathered around him.

'Look, this isn't ethical,' one of the men said. 'Get that man up again.'

'Sure — but not right now.' Drygulch

tugged out his gun. 'Don't any of you boys start undoin' my work or there's goin' to be trouble. Fergit yore rangers fur a moment an' behave like ordinary men. This skunk on the end ov a rope is a dirty killer, a hold-up man, and a destroyer of property. Yuh want a confession out of him, and I want to make him smart fur beatin' me up. Way I've got things figgered we c'n both be satisfied. F'r instance . . . '

Drygulch looked down into the depths where the sickened Dyson was still spinning, then he called to him:

'Listen, sheriff. It's up ter you now. Yore going to be asked some questions and when you answer 'em you can come up. If yuh don't yuh'll go down. I'm cutting this rope strand by strand fur every second yuh delay in answering. Now git busy.'

Abe hesitated for a brief moment and then stepped forward.

'Feather-Fist Jones here, Dyson. Up to now you've denied all responsibility for the murder of Sylvia Drew. Time

240

you admitted the truth, isn't it?'

'Go to hell!' came Dyson's panting voice.

For response Drygulch picked up a chunk of stone and brought it down hard against the taut rope. To Dyson the jerk felt like a strand giving way.

'One second!' Drygulch called out, and then he walloped again. 'Two seconds — '

'Hold it! Hold it!' Dyson yelled frantically. 'Okay, it's right! It was me who shot at the dame — I didn't mean t'kill. It just happened. For God's sake get me away frum here!'

'Satisfied?' Abe asked briefly.

The three rangers looked at each other in the starlight before one of them answered.

'I suppose one could say that Dyson is speaking under duress, but I guess it's a confession just the same. Okay, drag him up.'

'A moment — ' Abe interrupted. 'There's Lynch Corbett too — every bit as bad as Dyson. Hey, Dyson, where's

Lynch Corbett? And answer quick!'

Silence, and a thud on the rope.

'He's — he's dead!' Dyson gasped back, half fainting.

'How did it happen?'

'In — in the saloon in that fight. Your men shot him.'

'That the *truth*?'

Silence again. Drygulch shrugged and thumped the rope.

'There won't be no strands left in a moment,' Dyson yelled. 'Fur God's sake give me a chance — All right, I shot him! I've only got one life yuh can take, haven't I?'

'That's enough,' the ranger nearest Abe said curtly. 'Drag him up. There's enough pinned on to him, along with these confessions before witnesses, to swing him nice and high — for good.'

★　★　★

And so it proved. Within a month the Tucson authorities had convicted and dispatched Dyson, after which Abe was offered the opportunity to join the ranks of the regular marshals. With the knowledge of the bonanza he had discovered he declined and instead preferred to assume a life of wandering with Drygulch, until the time came for the old man to take the last trail.

'I look at it this way,' Abe explained, to old man Drew, as he took his leave of him. 'The gold I've found makes me independent for life. I can go where I want and do what I want. What I *would* have done had dear Sil been here is a forgotten story. All I know now is I can't settle — not even in Mountain's End where they're so busy rebuilding. So I'll just keep going, taking a sweet memory with me.'

Abe felt in his pocket and produced the fragment of Courage Stone.

'At least I found how to be a man,' he said. 'Amazin' what a bit of stone can do.'

'It didn't,' Drew said quietly, and Abe stared at him.

'Didn't? But Sil told me — '

'Yes, I know what she told you. You got courage because you loved her, Abe, and because she loved you. Something of her own personality went into yours and gave you courage. That bit of stone is just ordinary rock. The rest was your own mental attitude — and hers. She chose a visible means in the belief it would help you more.'

Abe smiled faintly, then he tossed the fragment into the open firegrate.

'Somehow,' he muttered. 'I always suspected. At least I shall always have *something* she gave me, and what more can a girl give a man than the courage to fight for himself?'

We do hope that you have enjoyed reading this large print book.

Did you know that all of our titles are available for purchase?

We publish a wide range of high quality large print books including:
Romances, Mysteries, Classics
General Fiction
Non Fiction and Westerns

Special interest titles available in large print are:
The Little Oxford Dictionary
Music Book, Song Book
Hymn Book, Service Book

Also available from us courtesy of Oxford University Press:
Young Readers' Dictionary
(large print edition)
Young Readers' Thesaurus
(large print edition)

For further information or a free brochure, please contact us at:
Ulverscroft Large Print Books Ltd.,
The Green, Bradgate Road, Anstey,
Leicester, LE7 7FU, England.
Tel: (00 44) 0116 236 4325
Fax: (00 44) 0116 234 0205

Other titles in the
Linford Western Library:

SPARROW'S GUN

Abe Dancer

Before setting off in pursuit of his father's murderers, Will Sparrow must learn how to handle a gun . . . Miles away from home, he plans his reprisal while working as a stable-boy. But then Laurel Wale happens along, and Will discovers his intentions aren't quite as clear-cut as he thought . . . Meanwhile, his mother has settled down nearby with one of the territory's most important citizens. She wants nothing more than peace — but nothing is going to deter Will from his fateful objective.

BLACKJACKS OF NEVADA

Ethan Flagg

Five years in prison have given Cheyenne Brady plenty of time to dwell on revenge after being left for dead during a hold-up by the Nevada Blackjacks. Upon his release Brady joins up with an old prospector, Sourdough Lamar; together they head for Winnemucca and the prospect of honest work. But when Brady's old gang, led by Big-Nose Rafe Culpepper, plans to rob the town's bank, Cheyenne is accused of masterminding the hold-up. Can he extricate himself from once again sinking into a life of crime?

INCIDENT AT FALL CREEK

D. M. Harrison

As Charles Gilson's line of employment usually involves wanted dodgers and a sawn-off shotgun, when he receives news of an inheritance, he is determined to make a fresh start. But Gilson has competition for the money: Theodore Alden has charged his lawyer with securing it by fair means or foul. With everyone, including Town Marshal Hardy, against Gilson, the odds seemed stacked against him — it will take more than a few bullets to secure what is rightfully his . . .

WHITE WIND

C. J. Sommers

Spuds McCain is convinced the White Wind brings disaster to all those who sense its message. Hobie Lee is sceptical. But bad things do happen to the Starr-Diamond Ranch — Hobie is hoodwinked and ambushed into trouble when his charge, Ceci Starr, disappears on a trip to town. The White Wind blows away the rest of his common sense as he determines to restore the reluctant Ceci to her father: it will take a maelstrom of death and double-cross before it blows itself out and Hobie can find peace.

BACK FROM BOOT HILL

Colin Bainbridge

After finding himself inside a coffin on the way to Boot Hill, Clay Tulane wants answers. Whilst local towns-folk Miss Winona and the boy Pocket help him piece together the story of how he got there, Tulane finds him-self drawn into a violent struggle against local landowner Marsden Rockwell and his Bar Nothing outfit, who want to take over the neighbouring Bar L. As tension mounts, the search for the truth throws up many more ques-tions . . .